Whatever After

GENIE IN A BOTTLE

Read all the **Whatever After** books!

Whatever After

GENIE IN A BOTTLE

SARAH MLYNOWSKI

Scholastic Inc.

Copyright © 2016 by Sarah Mlynowski

This book was originally published in hardcover by Scholastic Press in 2016.

ISBN 978-0-545-85103-9

10 9 8 7 6 5   20 21

Printed in the U.S.A.   40
First printing 2017

for maddie and molly wolf
cousins and sweeties

chapter one

Penny's Pennies

You've already read twenty books?" I ask. "That's amazing."

"Thanks, Abby," says my best friend Frankie. We're sitting at a crowded table in the cafeteria, eating lunch. "How many have you read?"

"Only nine," I say, and take a bite of my cheese sandwich.

"That's still great." Frankie nods and adjusts her cute red-framed glasses. Her twenty-first book is on the table, next to her blueberry yogurt.

This month, the fifth grade is doing a read-a-thon. That means that we have to get our parents to pledge a certain amount of money for every book we read, and all the money we raise goes to help our school library. My parents and Frankie's parents both pledged two dollars a book, which means that I've made eighteen dollars so far. Frankie has raised forty! The person who raises the most money gets to help the librarian pick the books that the library should order. Tomorrow is our deadline.

If I win — and, um, it's not looking promising — I know exactly which books I'm going to ask for: more books about fairy tales. The library has three fairy tale books now, but last week when I went to find one, all of them were checked out. I think the third grade is doing a unit on fairy tales. Great for them, but does that help me? Not at all.

Why am I obsessed with fairy tales? Because I go INTO them. I do! Pinkie swear. So far, I've visited *Snow White*, *Cinderella*, *The Little Mermaid*, *Sleeping Beauty*, *Rapunzel*, *The Snow Queen*, *Beauty and the Beast*, and *The Frog Prince*. I never get to choose the story. I don't even know the fairy tale I'm going to end up in until I'm in it. Which is why I need more fairy tale books to be available in the library.

It's very, very helpful when I've read the tales and know what's going to happen next.

Yeah, I can ask my parents to buy me more books about fairy tales, but they don't know about the magic mirror and I don't want them to get suspicious. They've already almost caught me and my little brother, Jonah, coming back from some fairy tales. They're lawyers, and pretty smart.

HOW do my brother and I go into fairy tales? Well, we have a magic mirror in our basement. If we knock on the mirror three times at midnight, *poof* — we step right inside a story.

Really.

See, there's a fairy named Maryrose who is trapped in our mirror and she's the one who takes me and Jonah inside. We're not sure why she's trapped, but we do know she was cursed. We're also not sure why she sends us into the stories she does. All we know is that she has some sort of mission for us. I kinda think our mission is to help uncurse her, but I don't know for sure.

"Are you going to read any more books by tomorrow?" Frankie asks me, and I snap back to the present.

"I'm hoping to finish the one I'm reading," I say. "Then I'll be at ten." I've been reading everywhere. At home. At recess. In the car on the way to and from school. I even read twenty-two pages in the bathtub last night, which may not have been the best idea since I sort of dropped the book in the tub. Anyway. It's still readable. Damp, but readable.

I turn to Robin, my other best friend. "What about you?"

"I've read five," she says, glancing up from her book and her turkey sandwich. Her strawberry-blond hair is pulled back in a high ponytail. "But my parents pledged three dollars a book, so I've already raised fifteen dollars. Woot!"

Robin is super smart at science but not the fastest at reading and writing, so I'm glad her parents are giving her an extra reward.

"I didn't mean to interrupt your reading," I say with a wave of my hand. "Go, go, go!"

"I've only read one book," offers Penny from across the table. She makes a face. "I hate reading."

"Well, I guess you won't get to be the one to pick out the books," I say. Okay, that was a bit mean. But Penny isn't exactly my favorite person. Robin, Frankie, and I are a set. We're all three best friends. But Penny is Robin's *other* best friend, which is why she's sitting with us. Penny has her hair in a high ponytail, just like Robin's. They like to be twinsies. It's annoying.

Penny pops a grape in her mouth. "Actually, I probably will. My parents pledged a hundred bucks."

What? "A hundred bucks?" I repeat. "How many books do you have to read for that?"

"One," Penny says, twirling her pony. "They're going to donate a hundred bucks no matter what. And I've already read one. So I get a hundred."

My jaw drops. Her parents are giving her a hundred dollars? For reading one book? That's the craziest thing I've ever heard.

I wonder if I can get my parents to do the same thing.

She laughs. "Maybe I could bring in a hundred dollars in pennies. Penny's pennies. How hysterical would that be?"

Ten thousand pennies would be heavy, not hysterical. And super annoying.

"I hope I can pick out fashion magazines instead of books," Penny goes on. "Or maybe I'll get lots of books about horses."

Penny loves horses. Her cubby is covered with pictures of Thoroughbreds.

I cannot let that happen. I cannot let all the new stuff be

fashion magazines or books about horses. I will not be able to free Maryrose while galloping into fairy tales and looking stylish.

Here's the thing: If I win the read-a-thon, I'm not *only* asking the librarian to order more fairy tale books. I'm also asking her to order a book on spells and curses. And with a book on spells and curses — and how to reverse them — I can help free Maryrose from our mirror. So I *have* to win.

"Mom? Dad?" I say at dinner. "Would you guys give me more money for my read-a-thon?"

"How much more?" my mom asks, passing me the bowl of mashed potatoes.

I do the calculations in my head. I'm almost up to ten books, so . . . "What if you give me ten dollars a book?" I suggest. That would get me to one hundred! No. Wait. Then Penny and I would be tied. "Ten dollars and one cent per book?" That would get me to one hundred and ten cents. I'd win!

"Honey, that's a lot of money," my mom says. "I think two dollars a book is a good motivator to keep you reading."

I've lost my appetite. "But it's not enough! I'm going to lose."

"I think you're forgetting the point of this read-a-thon, Abby. It's not to win. It's to help the library," my dad says, taking a bite of his roast beef.

I sink into my chair. I know they have a point. But they don't get it.

Jonah is making wells in his mashed potatoes instead of coming to my defense. Hello? Doesn't he know how important this is?

Except he doesn't. I haven't told him about my plan to order a book on spells. But I can't say anything now, in front of our parents.

A glob of mashed potatoes falls off my brother's fork and lands on his place mat.

Our dog, Prince, jumps up out of nowhere and licks it off.

"No, Prince, get down!" Jonah says sternly. Prince has been acting up lately. A lot. Last week he chewed up my mother's new sneakers. He also jumped on my desk chair and used his snout to knock the read-a-thon books off my desk. Over the weekend, he stole my dad's meatball sandwich. Yesterday he ate Jonah's math assignment.

Okay, it's possible my brother made that last one up. He probably just didn't do his homework.

But anyway, my parents put my brother in charge of training Prince in manners. So far, Prince's grade is an F.

"If you don't stop," Jonah tells him, "I'm putting you in the other room."

Prince hangs his head. But I think he's just pretending, because he's happily licking the potatoes off his doggy lips at the same time.

Jonah is doing about as well with his dog training as I am with my read-a-thon.

That night I stay up late reading my tenth book, *Wishing Day*. But I'm distracted. Despite it being a great book, I've been reading the same page for the past fifteen minutes. I yawn. Should I push myself and try to finish it tonight?

What's the point?

I'm still going to lose. I will not make more money than Penny. I will not win the read-a-thon. I will not convince the librarian to order a book on spells and curses.

I look at the clock. It's 11:40 P.M.

Maryrose lets us through the mirror only at midnight. That's twenty minutes away.

Since I'm not going to be able to help her here, I might as well see if there's any way to uncurse her by going through the mirror. At least there's magic in the fairy tales, unlike here in Smithville.

I slam my book shut and sit up.

I know what I have to do.

chapter two

Operation Help Maryrose

I put on my jeans, a yellow T-shirt, a blue zip-up sweatshirt, and my running shoes. Since I never know which fairy tale we're going into, I have no clue what to wear. Will I need a bathing suit? Or a snowsuit? A snowsuit would totally have been useful in *The Snow Queen*. It was freezing. Tonight, I am going with just a regular outfit and hoping for the best.

I look around for my newish watch. I need to wear my watch when I go into fairy tales. It keeps track of the time back home in Smithville. Time in fairy tales passes differently. Sometimes a day in a fairy tale is an hour at home. Sometimes two hours in a fairy tale is one hour back home. We never know until we're there.

I walk over to my jewelry box on my dresser. The box is decorated with drawings of fairy tale characters. Like Snow White. But this Snow White is wearing my pajamas. That's because Jonah and I always mess up the fairy tales we enter. The characters on my jewelry box change to show what happens after Jonah and I return home. I smile at the princesses, open the box, and grab my watch.

I ease open Jonah's door and gently shake him awake. "C'mon! Let's go through the mirror and see if we can help Maryrose," I whisper.

Prince jumps onto my brother's bed. Then he chomps down on the stuffed lion Jonah has had forever and starts shaking it like crazy.

"Prince, no!" I grab the lion out of his mouth. Ew, it's all slobbery.

"Maybe we should leave Prince here as punishment," Jonah says, frowning at his mangled stuffed animal.

I snort-laugh. "As if that would work. He'll bark the whole time and wake Mom and Dad! He comes with us."

Ruff! Prince says, heading for the door.

"But what if Prince does something super bad in whatever fairy tale we end up in?" Jonah asks, getting out of bed. "Maybe we should wait until he stops acting up."

Thud. Thud. Thud. I hear paws racing down the stairs. Prince is already heading for the basement.

"We can't wait!" I argue. Okay, we could probably wait till tomorrow, but I really want to go now. When I find out that Penny won the read-a-thon by reading ONE book, I'll feel less like a loser if I know I did something even more important than win a read-a-thon — like help a cursed fairy.

Jonah quickly puts on his favorite sweatpants, a blue T-shirt, and sneakers. Then we run downstairs. Prince is waiting for us at the door to the basement. I open it and the three of us fly down the final steps.

Right in front of us is the magic mirror. It's about twice the size of me. The outside is made of stone etched with drawings of little fairies and wands. The glass part is smooth.

All of a sudden, I yawn a giant yawn.

Jonah tilts his head. "You sound tired."

I yawn again but stop myself in the middle. "I'm not

tired! I'm fine!" Okay, so maybe I've been up late reading a lot, but I'll be all right. "C'mon! Maryrose is in trouble! Let's go!"

I don't waste any more time. I knock once. There's the usual hissing sound.

I knock a second time and the room fills up with a purple haze.

In the reflection, Prince's brown fur looks purple. So does Jonah's wavy dark hair and pale skin, and *my* curly dark hair and pale skin.

"Get ready!" I say, and knock a final time.

Our purple reflections start to swirl.

And Prince leaps straight through the mirror.

"Prince, wait!" I cry.

But does he wait? Nope!

I grab Jonah's hand and we jump in.

Going through the mirror never hurts. It feels like you're stepping through an open door.

I'm expecting to land on grass. Most of the fairy tales we visit take place in a forest. I am often wiping grass and leaves off my clothes.

So I'm kind of surprised when I land in the middle of a dirt road.

BONK!

Ouch! Something just conked me on the side of the head. Maybe sometimes going through the mirror *does* hurt.

chapter three

Duckball

I rub my head. Ow. Ow. Ow.

"Sorry!" someone calls.

I look to my left. There's a teenage boy with dark hair, big dark eyes, olive skin, and a Band-Aid on one knee. He's holding a half-flattened ball.

"Are you okay?" he asks. "I'm so sorry you got hit."

"I'm okay," I tell him. I glance at Jonah, who's sitting beside me, but he apparently did not get bonked in the head. He's looking around and grinning.

"I think we're in *Jack and the Beanstalk*," he whispers to me.

I doubt that. Johah always thinks we're in *Jack and the Beanstalk*.

"Bet you can't get me!" another boy calls out in a singsong voice. "Bet you can't!"

The nice teenage boy throws a ball at the other boy and hits him on the arm.

"You got me," the other boy says, frowning. He moves to the side and sits down with a bunch of other kids.

Uh, did we just land in a fairy tale gym class? I look around. There are about six kids, all a little older than me. They're wearing shorts and T-shirts, and they're sweaty. We're not near any kind of school or playground, but on a narrow road. There's a low stone wall off to the side and small stone houses all close together. The sky is bright blue and the sun is *hot*.

I'm *so* glad I didn't wear a snowsuit.

"Can you guys get out of the way?" a girl with a dark brown ponytail yells at me.

"Sorry!" I say, and scramble to stand up. I wonder what game the kids are playing. Something magical? Something we've never heard of because they only play it in fairy tale lands? "Jonah, come on! Prince? Where are you?"

16

I hear a *ruff.* Prince is eyeing the ball.

"No, Prince," I say. "It's not yours!"

He doesn't listen and lunges for it.

"Prince, no!" Jonah says. "Uh-oh, Abby. I didn't bring any of his training treats."

I jump up and grab on to Prince just as he's about to bite into the ball. Prince loves to play catch, which sometimes causes problems in fairy tales, even when he's on his best behavior. When we were in *The Frog Prince,* he lunged after the golden ball and that caused the whole story to unravel.

I look for the right person to throw the ball back to. "What's your game called?" I ask the girl with the brown ponytail. "Magicball? Goldenball? Fairyball?"

"Duckball," says a girl.

"Cool," I say. "Are there ducks involved? Do they fly? Is there magic?"

"No," she says. "If you hit someone with a ball and they don't catch it, they're out."

"Oh! It's dodgeball!" Jonah says.

How boringly regular.

"I love dodgeball!" Jonah continues. "I'm really good at it! I won my tournament today!"

"Do you guys want to play?" asks the nice boy with the Band-Aid on his knee.

"Yes!" Jonah exclaims just as I say, "No!"

Jonah turns to me with a pout. "Why not?"

"Really?" I ask. I resist rolling my eyes. "You don't know why not?"

"Fine," Jonah grumbles. "Thanks anyway," he says to the group of kids and then follows me and Prince to the low stone wall. I hear him mutter, "You're no fun," under his breath.

"Until we figure out where we are," I remind him, "just look, watch, and don't touch. You know we can't just pop into a story and mess it up."

"Yes, we can," Jonah says. "We always do!"

That's true. Usually we mess up the story by accident. Like when we accidentally broke Cinderella's glass slipper.

Or when Prince caught the golden ball.

"And anyway, that's why we're here, isn't it?" Jonah asks. "To help Maryrose? The only way we're going to help Maryrose is by messing the story up."

"That's not true," I say. "The way we're going to help Maryrose is by finding a way to uncurse her. And anyway,

18

we have to be careful — we don't even know what story we're in yet!"

"I'm telling you, it's *Jack and the Beanstalk*," Jonah says.

Jonah is obsessed. "You haven't actually read *Jack and the Beanstalk*, have you?" I ask.

"I have!" he says. He cocks his head to the side. "Maybe. I'm not sure."

I snort-laugh. "If you haven't even read it, why do you want to visit it?"

"Because I know it has giants in it! And climbing! And it's not a princess story! We are always falling into princess stories. Would it kill us to climb into a giant's story?"

"Hey, I don't choose the fairy tales," I say with a shrug. "I just fall into them. Take it up with Maryrose."

"I will if she talks to us again," Jonah says. He looks around once more. "So where do you think we are?"

"Um . . ." I'm really not sure. There's definitely no fairy tale about duckball. At least not one that I've ever heard of. "What fairy tales have balls in them?"

"Oh!" Jonah cheers. "Cinderella?"

I laugh. "Not that kind of ball."

He giggles. "Duh. I guess the *The Frog Prince*. But we were just in that one."

Prince barks.

We watch as one of the duck/dodgeballs goes flying in the air. The nice boy who apologized to me catches the ball with one hand.

"Catchers keepers!" he yells.

The girl with the ponytail cheers. "Good catch, Aladdin!"

Aladdin?

Aladdin!

chapter four

Look Out!

did you hear that, Jonah?" I whisper excitedly.

"That she called him Aladdin?"

"Yes! Do you know what that means?"

He squints at me. "That his name is Aladdin?"

"Yes. And that means that we're in the story of . . ." I wait for him to figure it out.

He bites his lip and thinks for a moment. *"Jack and the Beanstalk?"*

"Jonah!" I slap my palm against my forehead.

"I'm kidding, I'm kidding," Jonah laughs. "It's the story of

Aladdin. Probably. Unless Jack has a friend named Aladdin. That's possible, too."

"Possible," I say. "But unlikely. We're in the story of *Aladdin*."

"Fun!" Jonah rocks back and forth on his heels. "I want to ride a magic carpet! Where are the magic carpets?"

Prince starts wagging his tail. I guess dogs like the sound of flying carpets, too. Who doesn't?

"Um . . . I have bad news," I tell Jonah. "There are no magic carpets in the original story."

"What?" he asks, deflating like a two-day-old balloon. "No magic carpets? How can that be?"

"Well, there are flying carpets in other stories in *The Thousand and One Nights*, but not in the story of *Aladdin*."

Jonah frowns and kicks at a little rock on the ground. "But . . . but . . . what's the point of being in *Aladdin* if we can't ride a magic carpet?"

"There are other magic things," I say. "Like a magic lamp! And a magic ring!"

Jonah looks doubtful. "Do they fly?"

"Not exactly," I admit.

"You better tell me the whole story," he says. He hoists

himself up on the stone wall. "Guess I should make myself comfortable."

Prince curls up below Jonah's dangling feet and closes his eyes.

Now I just have to remember the tale. My nana read us stories from *The Thousand and One Nights* over the years. And I read some of those stories recently myself — including the one about Aladdin.

That's one of the books our school library *does* have. But their version is called *The Arabian Nights* and only includes some of the stories.

"Here goes," I say to Jonah. "Once upon a time, there was an evil magician."

"Jafar!" Jonah says. "I remember him from the movie about Aladdin!"

"That's not his real name," I say. "That's just his name in the movie. The movie is pretty different from the real story. In the book, I think he was just called Evil Magician. So, the evil magician heard about a magic lamp with amazing powers. Of course he wanted it for himself, but he needed someone else to get it for him."

I yawn. I wish I'd gotten more sleep the past few days.

"Anyway," I continue, "the evil magician sees Aladdin and tells him that if Aladdin does him a favor, he'll make Aladdin rich and successful. So they go through the desert until they get to a cave."

Jonah raises his hand. "And you're sure they don't go through the desert on a magic carpet?"

Did I not already tell him there is no magic carpet? I ignore the question.

"Once they're at the cave, the evil magician gives Aladdin his magic ring to wear. Aladdin puts the ring on and then descends into the cave. It's scary, but there are also jewels hanging on trees like fruit. Aladdin takes some jewels and then finds the lamp. He goes back to the mouth of the cave and tells the evil magician that he has the lamp. The magician tells him to pass it up to him and then he'll help him out of the cave."

Jonah tenses up. "That sounds so sketchy! I don't trust the evil magician at all!"

"Good! You shouldn't! He was planning on taking the lamp and closing the cave around Aladdin. But! Aladdin thought he was being sketchy, too. So he refused to give up the lamp until the evil magician helped him out. The magician got so mad he closed the cave on Aladdin!"

"Oh, no!"

"So Aladdin is stuck in the cave. But then he accidentally rubs the ring and a genie pops out!"

Jonah's mouth drops open. "I thought the genie was in the lamp?"

"Yes. But this is *another* genie."

His eyes light up. "How many genies are there?"

"Two. So of course Aladdin asks to be wished out of the cave. Then when he gets back to his house, his mother tries to clean the lamp — and a genie pops out of that, too."

"The real one!"

"Yup. Aladdin wishes for some food. And food appears! And fancy plates! It's great. Anyway, one day Aladdin accidentally spies the princess."

Jonah scratches his knee. "Jasmine? Or is that only her name in the movie?"

I hoist myself up on the stone wall next to Jonah. "Only her name in the movie. In the story, it's Badr-al-Badur. And Aladdin falls madly in love with her. Aladdin's father had passed away, but his mother goes to the sultan, the princess's dad, to ask if Aladdin and the princess can get married. The sultan says that Aladdin has to bring him forty buckets filled with jewels. Forty buckets! Impossible, right? The sultan doesn't expect Aladdin to make that happen because Aladdin's mom looks poor. But Aladdin has the genie of the lamp! Who has super-strong magic! And the genie makes it happen! And then the sultan has no choice but to agree to the marriage."

"So they get married? And live happily ever after?"

I shake my head. "Not yet. First Aladdin gets the genie in his lamp to build a beautiful palace for him and the princess to live in. But then the evil magician reappears and tricks the princess into giving him the magic lamp."

"Oh, no!"

"The lamp genie pops out and has to grant the evil magician's wish: that the new palace be moved to the other side of the world — along with the princess!"

Jonah's eyes widen. "Yikes."

"Yikes is right. But then Aladdin remembers his magic ring. He rubs it and asks the ring genie to send him over to the palace. When Aladdin finds the princess there, he tells her to put poison in the evil magician's drink. It works. Aladdin takes the lamp and wishes them and the palace back home."

"And then they live happily ever after?"

"Well, some more stuff happens, but yes, they do," I say.

"So *now* can I go play duckball?" Jonah asks. "Prince is being good. Look."

I glance down at Prince. He's napping. I yawn again. I wish I could take a nap.

I look over at the game. It does actually look like fun. "Okay, fine. Go ahead."

"Yay!" Jonah says, and runs over to Aladdin.

"I can play, right?" Jonah asks him.

Aladdin smiles. "Sure. But I'm pretty good, so watch out," he says, and whams the ball at Jonah. But not that hard, I notice.

Awww, Aladdin really is a nice guy.

Jonah catches the ball and throws it at a boy. The ball bounces off his leg and hits a girl in the stomach.

The girl doubles over and at first I think she's hurt, but she's laughing. "Guess I'm out," she says, and tosses me a ball.

Oh, why not? I AM pretty good at dodgeball. I just hate the getting-hit-with-the-ball part.

"Try to get me!" Aladdin calls to me, grinning. I grin back and throw the ball as hard as I can and —

Oops. The ball hits him right in the face.

GULP. His nose is bleeding!

Oh, NO!

"I am SO sorry!" I say, rushing over to him. "Are you okay?"

Jonah runs over to us, too, looking worried.

The rest of the kids stop playing and gather around.

"I'll be okay," Aladdin says, covering his nose with his hand. But he doesn't look that okay. "I'll just run home for an ice pack. You guys keep playing!"

The rest of the kids start the game again, but Jonah and I head back over to the stone wall, watching as Aladdin dashes off down the road.

"I feel terrible," I say. I started off wanting to help Maryrose and now I've ended up HURTING Aladdin!

"Did we mess up the story?" Jonah whispers fearfully.

My stomach tightens. "I don't know," I admit. "I hope not."

"Hey," Jonah says, standing up on the wall. "Who's that?"

I grab his hand and yank him back down. Does he want to end up with a bloody nose, too?

"Who?" I ask.

Then I notice that a man has appeared on the road and is watching the duckball game. He looks to be about my dad's age. He has piercing gray eyes and gray hair, and is tall but rail thin. He's wearing shimmery copper clothes and a shimmery copper cape. His shoulders are hunched, his hands are clenched, and his shadow is looming over the kids.

"That guy looks kind of creepy," I say "Oh! I bet I know who he is."

"The evil magician!" Jonah and I say at the same time.

chapter five

The Evil Magician

I can't believe Aladdin would actually help that guy," Jonah says. "Um, hello! Hasn't he heard the term 'stranger danger'?"

Jonah and I watch as the evil magician studies the kids playing duckball, a frown on his face. He's clearly looking for someone.

Oh. Right.

He's looking for Aladdin. So he can bring Aladdin to the cave and make him find the magic lamp.

But Aladdin isn't here, because I gave him a nosebleed.

Oops.

"Um, Jonah?" I say.

"Yeah?" says Jonah.

"I think we — well, I — messed up the story."

Prince wakes up with a bark, as if he's heard me.

Quickly, I explain to Jonah how Aladdin WON'T be able to help the magician now, due to the bloody nose I gave him.

"But maybe that's a good thing!" Jonah says. "We don't want Aladdin getting mixed up with the evil magician anyway, right?"

I shake my head. "But Aladdin needs the genie if he's going to end up with the princess. We have to make this right!"

Ding ding ding! Suddenly, I have an idea. The story never says why the evil magician picks Aladdin to get the lamp. Maybe it can be any kid.

Maybe it can be . . . us.

"Hey, Jonah," I say. "What if *we* get the lamp? Then we'll give it to Aladdin later!"

Jonah looks at me like I'm nuts. He does that a LOT. "How?"

"You go up to the evil magician. Start talking to him. Then he'll take you!"

Jonah's eyes bug out. "Me? You're sending ME over to the evil magician? Have YOU ever heard of stranger danger?"

"He's not a stranger! We know who he is and exactly what is going to happen. He's the evil magician from the story!"

"Good point," Jonah says. "But doesn't the person who gets the lamp have to be Aladdin?"

"I don't think so. All the evil magician needs is *someone* to go get it. Someone who's willing to go inside the cave."

"Why doesn't the magician just go into the cave himself?" Jonah asks. "And if he's a magician, why can't he just work some magic to make the lamp appear in his hand?"

Forget the read-a-thon — if there was such a thing as a question-a-thon, Jonah would win it.

"I have no idea," I say.

Jonah's eyes light up. "But I'm totally willing to go in the cave. Do you think it has bats and stuff? Like a haunted-house cave?"

My back stiffens. Hmm. "Maybe this is not a good idea."

"No, it is a good idea," Jonah insists. "I've always wanted to go exploring in a cave." Then his whole face lights up. "Ooh. And I just thought of something else!"

"What?" I ask suspiciously.

"If we get the lamp . . . maybe we can make a wish to free Maryrose!"

I gasp. I can't believe I didn't think of it myself. Jonah is right! This is a brilliant plan. We'll be able to help out Aladdin AND Maryrose at the same time.

"It's perfect," Jonah continues excitedly. "I'll go in the cave, I'll get the lamp, meet the genie, and wish Maryrose free. Then we'll give the lamp to Aladdin and everything can go on the way it's supposed to. It's a win-win."

I nod. It *does* sound perfect. But I'm suddenly nervous. I can't just send Jonah into a place that might be dangerous. What if he doesn't come back? Aladdin was okay in the story, but Jonah's only seven.

"I'm so excited," Jonah exclaims. He jumps down from the wall and starts running toward the evil magician. Prince goes racing after him.

I hurry to catch up with my brother, but I'm not fast enough.

"Hi, Mr. . . . um . . . man," I hear Jonah say.

I bet he almost called him Mr. Evil Magician.

The magician tears his eyes away from the players and looks down at Jonah. If he's noticed Prince sniffing his shoe, he doesn't say anything. "Can I help you?" he asks.

"What do you think of the game?" Jonah asks.

"It seems interesting," the evil magician says.

Jonah shrugs his scrawny shoulders. "Yeah? It looks boring to me. What's the point in throwing a ball back and forth?"

The evil magician looks at Jonah. "You don't like to play ball?"

"Not really," Jonah says. "It's not exciting enough for me. I like adventures. I like exploring. I like *danger.*"

I hold my breath.

The magician raises an eyebrow. "You do?"

"Yup! I am so bored. What a boring day. I wish I had something exciting to do. La la la la."

The *la la la la* may have been pushing his luck.

"Well," the man says, "I might have a suggestion."

It's working!

Jonah feigns surprise. "You do? I love suggestions!"

I stifle a laugh. I step closer to them.

"It just so happens that I am about to embark on an adventure," the evil magician says.

"Really?" Jonah says, his eyes extra wide.

The magician nods. "I need to get something from a cave. Would you like to help me?"

Bingo! "I would!" Jonah cries. "I really would!"

"Let us leave at once," the magician says, and motions for Jonah to follow him.

"Great!" Jonah says. Then he winks at me and starts to follow the man.

Is he kidding me? Does he really think he's just going to walk away with an evil magician? Not on my watch.

"Wait!" I holler.

Jonah and the magician turn to me.

"Excuse me?" the magician says.

"I'm coming with you!" I call out.

Woof! Woof-woof! Prince barks.

"*We're* coming with you," I correct.

The man looks at Jonah. "Do you know that girl?" he asks. "And that creature?"

"Yep." Jonah nods. "She's my sister. And that's our dog, Prince."

I hurry up to them, Prince at my side. "I love adventures, too. And, um, danger. So does my dog."

The man raises his eyebrows at me. He's probably surprised that he doesn't have to put in that much effort. In the original story, the evil magician pretends to be one of Aladdin's many uncles. He also sucks up to Aladdin's mother and even brings Aladdin fancy clothes before getting Aladdin to agree to come with him. This time he didn't have to do anything and he gets two kids *and* a dog.

"I really want to come," I add. "And Prince won't be any trouble. He's a good dog. Aren't you, Prince?" I give Prince a serious warning look. He *better* be good.

Ruff, Prince says extra sweetly.

"I suppose you can join us," the evil magician says. "Follow me."

Behind the man's back Jonah and I give each other a high five.

chapter six

The Cave

much to Jonah's dismay, we do not take a flying carpet to get to the cave. Instead, we walk. Far.

Really far.

We walk down the road and pass the small, cramped houses. Then we walk through an open-air market, where all kinds of stuff is for sale, like fruit, veggies, meat, pillows, and multi-colored sheets, scarves, and rugs.

After the market, we walk down winding streets where we see bigger homes, also made of stone. Some have domes and stained-glass windows.

Forget the read-a-thon. I would win a *walk-a-thon* for sure.

We walk through a garden of tall yellow and red tulips and then take a break at a small fountain.

Meanwhile, the evil magician has not said one word. Not one.

"So what's your name?" Jonah asks him. Clearly he's afraid of calling him Mr. Evil Magician by mistake.

"Dracul," the evil magician says.

"Dracul?" I ask. "Like Dracula but without the A?"

"Yes," Dracul says.

Well. That shouldn't be too hard to remember.

"What do you like to do for fun, Dracul?" Jonah asks, stretching his arms behind his head.

"For fun?" Dracul repeats.

"Yeah! Do you swim? Or rock climb?"

I press my lips together hard to keep from laughing.

"No," Dracul says. "I do not."

"What do you like?" Jonah asks.

"Cats," he says. He glares at Prince. "I am not a dog person."

Prince shimmies backward a bit.

Dracul takes a granola bar out of his sleeve and starts to eat it.

"Do you have any more of those?" Jonah asks. "I'm kinda hungry."

"I guess," Dracul says. He takes out another one and hands it to my brother. "Would you care for one, too?" he asks me.

I probably shouldn't take food from strangers, but he's eating one and . . . well, I'm also kinda hungry.

After our snack, we get up and leave the fountain area. We walk through the golden-domed city gates. In the distance, there's sand as far as the eye can see. I think we're about to enter the desert.

Prince is slightly ahead of us, dashing through the sand, having a blast.

I am hot. And thirsty. And getting blisters. Plus, sand isn't so easy to walk through! Every time the wind blows, a little bit gets in my eyes. There are a few trees scattered here and there with thin trunks and pointy-looking leaves, but there isn't much shade.

I check my watch. It says it's only 12:10 A.M. That's at home. We left home about two hours ago so time is moving much, much faster here than it is at home. But what time is it here? Clearly not the middle of the night. The sun is shining, but it's lower in the sky than it was when we got here. It must be late afternoon. Maybe around five?

What I *do* know: Jonah and I have to be home by six forty-five in the morning, when our parents wake up. Which means we still have some time to make our wish and fix the story.

Finally, about half an hour later, or two minutes in Smithville-time, according to my watch, Dracul comes to an abrupt halt.

"Here," he says with a wave of his hands. I don't see anything around us but more desert. "It's time for your adventure. But first I need to make a fire. Go get some branches."

Jonah and I head toward the trees, Prince following.

Jonah picks up a small branch. "Dracul's not much of a talker, huh?" he asks.

I grab a bunch of twigs. "He's probably too busy planning how to trap us in the cave once he gets the lamp."

"He doesn't scare me," Jonah boasts.

"He should! He scares me! Just remember: No matter what, we have to stay together."

Jonah picks up another branch. "I figured. But I totally could have done this on my own."

Sometimes my brother thinks he's seventeen instead of seven. "Do you really think it's a good idea for you to go into a magical cave by yourself?"

"Aladdin did it!"

40

"He's older than you!"

"But I'm a better duckball player," he insists. "I didn't get a bloody nose."

I sigh and scoop another stick off the ground. "C'mon."

We run back to where the magician is standing.

"Here you go," I tell Dracul, handing him the sticks.

Jonah hands over his, too. Prince has a stick in his mouth and drops it on the magician's foot. Awww! Prince is trying to be good.

Dracul sneers at Prince and kicks the drool-covered stick away.

Humph.

Dracul dumps the wood on the ground and leans over it, and suddenly, there's a small fire. Then he reaches into his pocket, takes out a handful of green powder, and flings it on the flames.

Dracul's gray hair has an eerie orange glow near the fire. I glance at Jonah. Jonah's eyes widen and he looks at me. Then we both look at the fire. What is going to happen?

"Magic collides, show us where the lamp resides," Dracul whispers.

Right in front of us, the flame expands into a huge circle of green fire.

Wow.

The ground beneath us shudders and shakes and I reach for Jonah's hand.

There is a lot of smoke at first, but when the smoke clears, there's a square stone hatch in the ground where there used to be sand. There's a gold ring attached to it. I guess it's a door.

"What is that?" Jonah asks.

"Under the door is your treasure," Dracul says. "Are you ready to find it?"

Oh, yeah, we are. Because the minute we find that lamp, I can uncurse Maryrose. Well, the genie who lives in the lamp can do that. But I can wish it!

Jonah and I both nod, and Jonah pulls up the ring. The hatch lifts. Underneath, there are stairs.

"Wait," Dracul says. "You must listen carefully to my instructions."

Now he's giving instructions? He had the whole long walk to give us instructions!

Dracul's gray eyes gleam. "When you reach the bottom of the stairs, you will have to go through three large rooms. Do not touch anything in these rooms OR ELSE."

My eyes bug out. "Or else what?"

42

"OR ELSE!" he repeats, and wags his fingers. "So do not touch anything."

"But what if something touches us?" Jonah asks. "Like a cobweb. Or a branch. Or a beanstalk."

Dracul stares at Jonah. "Don't touch anything OR ELSE."

I glance at Jonah. He puts his hands at his side very stiffly. It's a start.

But what if Prince touches something? Does it count if it's a dog?

I decide not to ask. I'll just have to hope Prince behaves.

"After the three rooms," Dracul says, "you will find a lamp. Dump out the oil in the lamp, and then bring it back to me."

The lamp!

"Do I get to keep it?" Jonah asks.

Dracul narrows his eyes. "Of course," he says.

I give Jonah a warning look. Meaning he shouldn't say anything else. I don't want Dracul to get suspicious.

"Understood?" the magician asks.

"Understood," we say.

Dracul nods. "Now go."

"I have one more question," Jonah says. "Why don't you come with us?"

The evil magician shivers. "I'm claustrophobic. I hate small, closed spaces."

"Not me!" Jonah says. Then he hurries down the steps, Prince right behind him. I hesitate. I feel like we forgot something. But what?

I look back at Dracul. His hand glistens. Oh! The ring! We need the magic ring! He gave Aladdin the magic ring, so he should give it to us, too.

"Wait!" I say to the magician. "I'm a little nervous about the OR ELSE part. Do you have something that can protect us?" I ask.

He looks at me blankly.

"Like a charm?" I say. "Or a magical piece of jewelry?" Hint, hint.

"Oh," he says. "I can lend you my ring. It will protect you." He slides the ring off his finger and is about to hand it to me when he hesitates. "Maybe I should keep this."

Huh? No! He can't. We need it as protection just in case something goes wrong. I mean, we're not planning on giving Dracul the magic lamp. But what if he tricks us and gets it anyway? We need that ring!

"Why?" I ask.

"Just because." His eyes are raking over me, narrowing and widening. Does he suspect something?

"But . . ." That's not the way the story goes!

Dracul is not handing over the ring. Now what?

I guess we won't really need it once we have the lamp. In the story, the genie of the lamp is much more powerful than the genie of the ring.

We only really need the genie of the lamp.

"Okay," I say. "Never mind. We'll just be super careful not to touch a thing. Except the lamp, of course."

I stare at him in case he changes his mind. He doesn't.

"All right, then," I say. "Off I go."

"Good-bye," he says. "Bring back the lamp."

Not going to happen, mister.

Obviously, I don't say that part. I head down the stairs. The stone steps wind down and down and down. Jonah is already ahead of me, but I don't want to hurry in case I slip. I can't see the bottom. It's a little nerve-racking.

There's an eerie green glow in the cave, so it's not too dark.

"Jonah?" I say, my voice echoing. "You there?"

"Wow," he says. "I'm in the first room! The walls are covered in mirrors!"

"Don't touch them!" I call out. "OR ELSE!"

"I know!"

"Keep your arms firmly by your side. In fact, clasp your hands together!"

"What if I trip and accidentally hit something?" he asks.

"Don't trip!"

"Abby? My shoelaces are undone."

"Tie them! Without touching anything!" Couldn't he have checked his shoelaces BEFORE entering a dark, super-creepy cave?

I finally come to the last step and see that Jonah was right. The room is about the size of our living room at home, and it's all mirrors. There are thousands of me everywhere! I raise my hand. All the me's raise their hands. I make bunny ears. All the me's make bunny ears.

"Abby, what are you doing?" Jonah asks, laughing.

"Uh, nothing," I say, seeing all the me's blush. "Did you tie your shoes?"

"Yup," he says.

All the Jonahs look like they have tied shoes. All the Princes let out a *Ruff! Ruff-ruff!* at their reflection.

46

"Don't touch anything, Prince," I tell our dog sternly. "Now let's go to room number two."

We walk through a narrow doorway, single file.

Room number two is completely black but filled up with giant stars. They hang in midair and from the ceiling, and float above the ground. Some are a few feet away from each other, some only a few inches.

"How are we supposed to get through this?" Jonah asks. "It looks like we're in a *Star Wars* movie!"

"Don't touch the stars," I say.

"But they're everywhere! They look like lasers!"

"I know. You have to be very careful. Prince, do not touch the stars!"

He woofs in response and starts zigzagging his way through.

Okay. The stars are all across the room in every direction. But there are spaces I can fit between — if I'm careful. Jonah's smaller, so he'll have even less trouble. I think. I hope.

I stare down the laser stars.

I can do this. No problem! I took gymnastics for three years!

I move forward. *Step. Bend. Arch*, I tell myself. *Step. Bend. Arch*.

I step. I bend. I arch. I'm around the first star! I got this. "Jonah, are you okay?"

"Finished!" he says. "Prince, too! He didn't touch a single star! Hey, where are you? I can't see you."

Phew about Prince. But how is Jonah done already? He never took gymnastics.

"I'm only past the first star!" I call out.

The truth is I never loved gymnastics because I'm not very flexible. *Step, bend, arch, SPLAT* was more how it went for me on the balance beam.

I'm around another star. Now on to the next. I step. I bend. I arch. I straighten my body and I . . .

"Ow!" I shriek.

I touched something. I touched a star with my elbow!

Oh, no! OR ELSE!

It burns. It really, really burns. It feels like hot ice digging into my skin.

"I touched a star!" I cry. "And it hurts!"

"Why did you touch it?" Jonah asks.

"By accident! Ow, ow, ow," I say as I continue bending and stretching my way over to him.

"Well, we know what the good news is," Jonah says when I reach him.

"What?" I ask.

"The OR ELSE wasn't that bad," Jonah points out. "Your arm didn't fall off. A cave monster isn't suddenly chasing us."

I rub my burning elbow. "That is good news."

We go through the door into the last room. This time, trees are everywhere, and they have fruit on them. All kinds of brightly colored beautiful fruits. Tiny apples. Tiny limes. Tiny pears. Tiny blueberries. Tiny white fruit that I can't identify. I look more closely. Are they fruit . . . or jewels? I remember something in the original story about there being jewels disguised as fruit in the cave.

"I think I'm going to take a few of these," I say. "In the story, Aladdin ends up needing jewels."

"What if they're burning hot, too?" Jonah asks.

GULP. I reach out and very quickly touch the back of my hand to a blueberry that looks like a sapphire.

"It didn't hurt!" I say. "I'm taking a few." I take a blueberry, a strawberry, and the white fruit. Oh! It's a lychee. The fruits are hard like gemstones and they sparkle. I put them in my pocket.

"Where's the lamp?" Jonah asks, looking around.

"It has to be in the next room," I say. "Keep walking."

We go into the next — and there's the lamp! It's on a small table with a purple tablecloth.

The lamp looks just as I imagined it would. Like . . . not a lamp. More like a kettle. It's dark gold and smooth and has a long spout. But light is coming from the center of it, so I guess it is a lamp.

"There it is!" Jonah says, pointing. "What do we do now?"

"We don't give it to Dracul, that's for sure. I guess we make a wish."

"Are you making the wish or am I?" Jonah asks.

"I will," I say. I step closer to the lamp. "Am I supposed to rub it?"

"I guess," he says. "Oh, wait! We're supposed to dump the oil."

I yawn. I'm so tired from staying up late that I'm forgetting important stuff! I pick up the lamp, but I don't see where the oil would be. I turn it upside down and some inky liquid spills out a little hole near the spout.

"Okay," I say. "Here goes —"

"Wait! Abby! What happens if it works?"

50

Huh? "Then it works. What's the problem?"

"We're going to wish for Maryose to get uncursed, right? Well, if she's not trapped in our mirror anymore, the mirror won't be magic! So how will we leave this fairy tale and get back home? We'll be stuck here."

Double huh. Jonah might be right about one thing: Our mirror might not be magic anymore if Maryose isn't in it. But that doesn't mean we'll be trapped in this fairy tale.

"We won't get stuck here," I assure him. "We'll have the genie, remember? He can help us get home."

"Good point," Jonah says, looking a lot less worried. "So," he adds, "do you think we could also wish for a magic carpet?"

Flying around on a magic carpet does seem like a fun way to get around. "I don't see why not. We can't bring it home, but I guess we could use it until we have to go back to Smithville."

"Yes!" Jonah exclaims, pumping his fist in the air.

"Okay," I say. "Time to make a genie appear."

chapter seven

Hello, Genie

I glance at Prince. "No barking at the genie, okay?"

Ruff! Prince agrees.

I touch the golden lamp with the tips of my fingers. It's warm and smooth-feeling. I rub my fingers against the side.

Jonah and I hold our breath.

Nothing happens.

I rub the lamp a little harder and then . . .

VROOM!

A huge cloud of sparkly gold dust bursts out of the spout, followed by a small, wrinkled old man with glasses. He's standing on the ground next to me, but I can see smoky-looking strings connecting him to the lamp. He reminds me of a puppet, but he's life-size. And hunched over.

"What do you want?" the man snaps. He's wearing what I can only describe as beige pajamas.

"Hel-l-l-o," I stammer. "Are you the genie?"

He snorts. "No, I'm the dentist."

"Huh?" I say.

"Yes, yes, yes. I'm the genie. Now I'm *your* genie. What do you want?"

"Oh. That was fast. Do I just say it?" My heart starts to hammer. This is so exciting! I get to make a wish! And it's going to come true! How amazing is this?

"I'm not great at reading minds," he says. "So yeah. You better say it."

Grrr-ruff! Grr-ruff! Prince barks. Oh, no! Prince is growling at the genie.

"Jonah, control Prince!" I say.

Jonah bends down and tells Prince, "No growling at the nice genie!"

I don't know if *nice* is the right word. The genie seems a little obnoxious.

"Are you sure I can't make the wish?" Jonah asks. "It was my idea."

"No. I'm doing it." I am still clutching the lamp. "Okay. Here we go —" I let out another giant yawn.

"Am I boring you?" the genie asks, one eyebrow raised.

"No!" I say. "Just tired. Sorry. I'm doing it now. We would like to uncurse our genie!"

He freezes. His eyes almost pop out of his wrinkled head. "You . . . would?"

"Yes!" I say.

"Are you sure?" He looks from me to Jonah. His expression is totally different now. From grumpy to . . . total shock.

"Yes," I repeat. "Is that all I have to do?" I ask. "Say it aloud?"

He nods multiple times. "You are incredible! Because of your age, I expected you to ask for something silly like a magic carpet, but no, you two are the best. The best, I tell you. The best! So noble and generous!" His eyes tear up.

"When do we ask for the magic carpet?" Jonah whispers in my ear.

"Not now, Jonah!" I whisper back. "He's about to do the spell!"

I puff up my chest and face the genie. "Why, thank you, genie. It's nice to be appreciated."

"Okay," the genie says. "Here we go, then." He sprinkles some of his sparkly dust over his shoulders and says, *"The world I shall return to thee; these children have set their genie free!"* His eyes are all misty and he presses both hands to his heart. "Thank you, thank you, thank you!" he cries. "You two kids have made me a very happy genie!"

Wait a minute. "I didn't say set my genie free!" I exclaim. "I said set my fairy free!"

"No, no, no! You definitely said genie."

"I did not!" I turn to Jonah. I suddenly have a bad feeling in the pit of my stomach. A lychee pit. "Did I?"

Jonah is very pale. "Abby," he says, "I think you did."

The strings connecting the genie to the lamp disintegrate into thin air.

"That jerk cursed me a thousand years ago, but now, finally, I'm free!" the genie cries. "Free!" He starts to shake his bum. "This is my happy dance! Look at me! I'm doing the happy dance!"

He was cursed a thousand years ago? He was cursed? And now he's uncursed?

"Sir," I say, "I'm so sorry, but I think we've had a tiny misunderstanding . . ."

He doesn't seem to hear. He is too busy doing his happy dance. Now he's shaking his bum, plus waving his arms above his head.

"Sir? Genie, sir?" Jonah says. "My sister didn't mean to uncurse you. She meant to uncurse Maryrose. The fairy living in the mirror in our basement. She just said the wrong word."

The genie freezes and turns to us. "You wished for me to be uncursed. Which means good-bye, lamp; good-bye, you!"

"But it was a mistake! I made a mistake!" I cried. "I meant to say fairy! I'm just tired! It's very late in Smithville! I had a stressful day!"

"Tough cookies!" he says. "I'm done. Out of here. Good-bye! Au revoir! Adios! Ma'a salama! Later, gators!"

"But — but — but!" I stammer.

Before I can say another word, the genie snaps his fingers and disappears.

chapter eight

Bye-Bye, Genie

t his is a problem," I say.

"It really is," agrees Jonah.

We're still standing in the cave and I'm still holding the lamp. The now empty lamp.

"I guess this means no flying carpet," Jonah says.

"It means more than that," I say. "It means we have no magic genie! If we have no genie, then we can't uncurse our genie."

"*Fairy*," my brother corrects. "Not *genie*."

Ugh. Drat. I did it again. I kick at the ground. "Right. Sorry. We can't uncurse our *fairy* Maryrose. And we have bigger problems than that. Without the genie of the lamp, the entire Aladdin story isn't going to happen. How is Aladdin supposed to get the princess to marry him if he's just a duckball-playing village guy? He can't! He's supposed to have all kinds of riches to win over her and the sultan." My heart starts beating really fast. "And without our genie, how are we supposed to get home?"

"On our flying carpet?" Jonah suggests.

"There is no flying carpet, Jonah! There is no magic at all! We are in serious trouble!"

"We can't really blame the genie, though, can we? You granted him his freedom. He took it."

Humph. I cross my arms over my chest. "I guess."

"And he was stuck in that lamp for over a thousand years," Jonah reminds me. "I'm sure he was pretty cramped."

"But what about us?" I ask. "What do we do now? We're stuck here in this cave!"

Jonah's face lights up. "Wait. But that's not true. There's the other genie, right?"

"What other genie?" I ask.

"You said there was another genie. The genie of the ring!"

Oh. Right! There IS another genie. The ring genie! "You're

right!" I was so mad at myself for messing up the wish that I forgot all about the other genie.

"And you got the ring from the evil magician, right?" Jonah asks.

Is it hot here? The back of my neck is getting sweaty. "Not exactly," I admit.

"But that's how it happens in the story! The magician gives Aladdin the ring before he goes into the cave to get the lamp. You were supposed to have the ring, Abby."

My day isn't going so well. "I tried, but he seemed to be getting suspicious and I didn't want to set off any alarm bells, so I didn't push it."

I kneel down on the rocky ground next to Prince. Crumbs! First I messed up my chance of uncursing Maryrose by not reading enough books in the read-a-thon. Then I messed up by hitting Aladdin in the nose. Then I messed up by wishing the genie free. Plus, I have no magic ring. No other magic genie is about to pop out and help us.

This is bad.

Jonah sits down next to me. Prince rests his furry chin on my knee.

"Aladdin did look like he was having fun playing duckball," Jonah points out. "At least he has that, even if he doesn't get his happily-ever-after. And I'm sure his nose stopped bleeding by now."

It's sweet of Jonah to try to make me feel better. But there's no way I'm keeping Aladdin from marrying the princess. And there's also no way I'm giving up on freeing Maryrose. I messed up and I'm going to unmess up. I just don't know how . . . yet.

"Let's go get the ring," Jonah says, standing up. He dusts off his pants. "Come on!"

I stand up, too. "How are we supposed to get it? Dracul isn't going to just hand over the magic ring to us."

Jonah smiles. "What if we trade it?" he asks.

"For what? All we have is an empty lamp," I say.

"But he doesn't know that!" Jonah says. "He sent us here to get the lamp, right? So we tell him that he can have the lamp if he gives us the ring!"

For a little brother, Jonah can be pretty smart. I nod and take a big breath. "Okay. Let's give it a try." I touch my elbow again. It still burns.

Which reminds me that the only way back to the mouth of the cave is back through the other rooms. I'm not looking forward to stepping, bending, and arching through those white-hot laser stars again.

"Let's go," I say. "Very, very carefully."

Unfortunately, I burn myself *again*. It's not on the same star, but in the *exact* same spot on my elbow. Ouch. We make it back to the stone steps leading to the mouth of the cave. I see Dracul. His copper cape shimmers in the late afternoon sun.

I clutch the lamp and climb up the stairs about three-quarters of the way. Jonah and Prince are right behind me.

"Hi there!" I call out. "We're back. I have good news!"

"You have the lamp?" Dracul asks, his gray eyes lighting up.

"I do! Isn't that great? We got it!"

His thin lips curve into a smile. "Good. Let me hold it for you, and then I'll help you out."

What a liar. That's what he promised to Aladdin when he was totally planning on leaving him to die down here. I don't feel at all bad that I'm about to trick him.

"Um . . . sure," I say. "I'll pass it over. But what are you going to give us in return?"

"Excuse me?" he asks, his tone turning cold.

I shiver. He's an evil magician and the one with the magic ring. I have to be very careful with what I say so that he doesn't trap us in the cave.

"It's an exchange, right?" I say. "You said there was treasure for us down here. But all we found was the boring old lamp you wanted. So we give you the lamp and you give us something."

"I told you about the cave!" he snaps. "That should be enough. You are ungrateful children!"

"No. We got the lamp for you. We risked our lives — our elbows! — to get the lamp. We want something in return."

"You can have another granola bar," Dracul says, pulling another one from his shirt pocket.

How many does he have in there exactly?

"We don't want more granola bars. We want" — I stare at the ring — "that," I say, pointing. "Your ring."

He backs up a bit, his gray eyes narrowing. "My ring?"

I nod and clutch the lamp against my stomach. "Yes. You give us the ring and we'll give you the lamp."

He leans his face closer to the opening of the hatch. "Why are you so obsessed with my ring?"

"Why are you so obsessed with the lamp?" Got you there, Mr. Evil Magician.

We stare at each other. I smile. "Final offer," I say. My heart races. If he says no, then we're really in trouble.

"Fine," he says with a sniff. "You can have the ring. It's worthless, though. Just a worthless old ring I've had forever." He stops, waiting for me to lose interest.

Sure, it is.

"Hand over the lamp first and then I'll give you the ring," he says, stretching out his long, thin, pale arm.

Is he kidding me? That's the same thing he tried with Aladdin. "I don't think so," I say. "Pass down the ring and then I'll hand up the lamp."

He hesitates.

"You want the lamp, don't you?" I call up.

"We'll hand them off at the same time," he says. "Deal?"

"Deal."

I reach my left hand up for the ring and hold the lamp with my right one. His left hand goes for the lamp while he shoves his right hand with the ring in my face.

"One. Two. Switch!" he says.

I take the ring. He takes the lamp.

Wahoo! "Got it!" I say, and very quickly march back down the stairs.

"Yes!" he cries. "Genie of the desert, you are now in my possession!"

"Should we run out now?" Jonah asks me.

"I don't know," I say. "He's going to be pretty angry any minute. Maybe better to hide out in here? He's claustrophobic. He won't come in."

I am standing at the bottom of the stairs when I hear Dracul yell:

"Hello, genie! I can't wait to meet you! Come out, come out wherever you are!"

We wait.

"Genie? What's wrong? Are you shy? Don't be. This is going to be great."

Still nothing.

"Do you want a granola bar?"

We snicker.

"Come on!" he yells. I can see him shaking the lamp. "Enough already! Get out! You have to listen to me! I'm your master!"

Now he's shaking the lamp upside down. "Wait a second . . . is this empty?"

Oh, it is. It definitely is.

"You miserable children! You ruined the lamp!" He throws more of his powder on the hatch and yells, *The lamp that you brought is useless; I will leave you here to rot!"*

Right in front of us, the hatch closes shut.

At first the cave feels really dark, but then my eyes adjust and I see little flickers of light.

"Abby!" Jonah says. "We're stuck! I told you we should have made a run for it!"

"It's okay," I say. I open my hand. A silver signet ring glistens in my palm. "I have the ring. Aladdin got out of here with this ring, and so will we."

chapter nine

Ring-a-Ding-Ding

b e careful this time, 'kay?" Jonah says.

"I will," I promise.

"Remember: Uncurse Maryrose, make Aladdin worthy of the princess, and get us home. Got it?"

"Shhh, you're distracting me."

Very, very carefully, I rub the side of the ring.

Poof! From the center of the ring, out comes a puff of sparkly purple haze, then I see the thin, smoky, dental-floss-like puppet strings again. The strings are attached to the ring . . . and to another genie.

A girl genie.

"Oh!" I say. "You're a girl!"

She stretches her arms above her head. "I am!"

"And you're young!" Not young like us, but like my mom when she was in college. Her pink hair is tied into a long braid down her back. She's wearing a silver one-piece jumpsuit and white sneakers.

"I'm a hundred and sixty," she says. "Not that young. But I *am* new at this. I've only been a genie for a hundred years or so. Before that, I was a kindergarten teacher."

"You can still grant wishes, though, right?" I ask hopefully.

She nods slowly. "Yes."

I clear my throat. I will be specific this time. And I will choose my words carefully. Very, very carefully. "We would like you to free Maryrose, the fairy who's trapped in our basement mirror in Smithville. Please uncurse her and set her free. Maryrose. Not you. Can you repeat what I just said to make sure that it's all clear? So we know we're on the same page."

The genie nods. "You want me to uncurse the fairy who lives in your basement mirror. So that she can be free."

"Yes," I say, relieved. "You got it." This is going to work! This is really going to work! We're going to free Maryrose! Yay us!

"Um . . . I can't do that," she says. The genie glances at Jonah and Prince. "Uh, hi."

"Hi," Jonah says. Prince sniffs her sneaker.

"What do you mean?" I ask. "Why not?"

She shrugs. "I'm just a baby genie. My magic isn't that strong yet. I can't reverse someone else's spell. Maybe in a hundred years or so . . ."

"We don't have a hundred years!" I look at my watch. It's 12:15 A.M. at home. Who knows what time it is here? "We have until six forty-five A.M.!"

She tilts her head. "What? It's only six P.M. right now."

Oh! Since we arrived three hours ago, at 3 P.M. here, that means every five minutes at home is one hour here. So we have some time. Not a hundred years, but still good!

"Can you get the other genie, the genie of the lamp, to come back?" Jonah asks.

The girl genie's bright yellow eyes widen. "Where did he go?"

I sigh. "We freed him. It was an accident."

"I can't make a powerful genie do what I bid!" she tells me. "You have to have tons of power for that."

I glance up the steps where a square little door used to be. "Okay. Can you open the hatch to the cave?" I ask.

The genie looks relieved. "Yes!" she says. "Probably. Is that your wish? To open the hatch?"

"Yes," I tell her. "That's my wish."

"Okay," she says. "Here goes nothing." She rubs her hands together and chants, *"Let the magic flow; it's time for us to go!"*

There's a burst of light from her finger. I feel a swirl of air around us that gets stronger and stronger and then — *pop!* The hatch bursts open.

"Wahoo!" I cry. "You did it."

She smiles, pleased. "I did!"

We all climb out of the cave. Ah, fresh air. I glance around to make sure the evil magician isn't lurking anywhere. I don't see him. Whew.

The genie's pink hair looks even pinker in the sunset.

"What's your name, anyway?" I ask her. "Are we just supposed to call you genie?"

"It's Karimah," she says.

"Hi, Karimah," I say. "Nice to meet you. I'm Abby and this is my brother, Jonah. That's our dog, Prince," I add. Prince is wriggling around the ground with his belly in the air.

Karimah smiles at Prince. "Pleasure to meet you all," she says.

Ow! My elbow has started to sting again.

Should I ask Karimah if she could make it stop hurting? I mean, she is a genie. And isn't her job to grant wishes?

"Karimah?" I say. "My elbow is really hurting. Can you help me?"

"I can try," she says. She scrunches her lips together and says, *"Magic that would, let your elbow feel good!"*

My elbow starts to tingle and then — presto! It stops burning.

"Hurrah!" I cry. "You did it."

Karimah beams.

"What else can you do?" I ask. "We have a whole list of stuff."

Her yellow eyes widen. "Can I see it?"

Oh. I laugh. "It's not an actual list. It's just in my head."

"Like, a magic carpet!" Jonah cries. "I wish for a magic carpet!"

"You're not holding the ring," Karimah tells him. "I can only grant the wishes of the person who has the ring!"

Jonah turns to me, his eyes all lit up. "Can I have the ring, can I have the ring?" he begs.

"I'm keeping the ring," I say. "I don't want you to lose it."

He frowns. "No fair! I haven't messed up anything all day!"

I flush. "True. I'm the one who messed up. And now it's my responsibility to make things right. The ring is our only way to save Aladdin's whole future AND free Maryrose AND get ourselves home. I can't take any chances with it."

Jonah makes his face all cute. "Then can you at least wish for a flying carpet? Pretty please?"

"Deal." I turn back to Karimah. "I wish my brother had a flying carpet."

Jonah jumps up and down. "Thanks, Abby! You're the best!"

Awww. It is pretty sweet that he still thinks I'm the best after all my mistakes today.

"Okay! I can do that," Karimah says. *"Carpet, carpet in the sky, carpet, let us see you fly!"*

A beautiful woven carpet appears right above the hatch. It has an intricate lilac-and-purple border with a gold medallion in the center. And it's hovering two feet off the ground. It reminds me of something, but I can't think of what.

"Hurrah!" Jonah cries. "A flying carpet! How cool is that?"

I have to admit it's pretty cool. But we need to focus here.

"We have to get back to Aladdin now," I tell Jonah. "We need to give him the ring." I glance at Karimah. "The genie of the lamp was supposed to do all kinds of magic spells for Aladdin. Like zap up a huge palace. Are you able to do that?"

"I'm not sure," she says with a shrug. "But I can try."

Great. She's much nicer than that lamp genie. "So my next wish is for you to take us to Aladdin's house!"

She frowns. "Oh, um. Well . . . I can't do that."

"What do you mean? Why not?"

"You already made three wishes," she says. "Three wishes is my limit."

"I thought that was just in the movie! I only get three wishes?"

"Yes. Three wishes. Per day."

Oh! That's not *that* bad. Have I already made three wishes? I wished for her to open the hatch. That was number one. I wished for my burning elbow to stop hurting. That was number two. I wished for . . . the flying carpet for Jonah! Grrr. Now what?

"So I can make another three wishes tomorrow?" I ask.

"Yup. No problem. And three more the day after that."

I'm not sure how many days we're going to be here exactly, but good to know.

"What if *I* take the ring? Can I get three wishes today, too?" Jonah asks.

"Nope. I can only do three in one day. Sorry. That's the way my magic works."

"Bummer," Jonah says. "But hey! Maybe we can take the flying carpet to Aladdin's!"

"We don't know where he lives," I point out.

"We know the way back to the place where he was playing duckball," he says. "We'll head there and try to find him."

I put the magic ring back on my finger. Karimah disappears.

Hey! "Where did she go?" I ask, looking around.

"Maybe that's how the ring works," Jonah says. "You take it off, rub it, and she appears. You put it back on, and poof, she goes back inside the ring."

Sounds about right. I make sure the ring is on tight. I don't want it falling off my finger while Jonah and I are riding the magic carpet.

"I'm climbing on!" Jonah exclaims. He throws himself at the carpet and sits up. "Do you talk?" he asks the carpet.

It does not respond.

"I guess not," he says, shrugging.

I step over and lift myself onto it, behind my brother. It wobbles underneath me. It feels a bit like a trampoline. "Okay, Prince, your turn. Jump on."

Prince does not move.

"Prince, you heard Jonah. Come on!"

Prince looks at me and lifts his leg to pee.

"Come on, Prince, be a good dog and jump on," Jonah says. "You can help me steer!"

Prince tilts his head, barks, and then jumps up onto the rug. He sits down in the center, right between me and Jonah.

"Okay, we're all aboard," I say. "Lead the way."

Jonah holds one arm straight out like he's Superman. "Go, carpet, go!"

It doesn't move.

"Hmm," he says. "It must not respond to voice commands. Maybe if I pull on one of the tassels?"

He pulls one of the tassels and we tilt to the right. I almost fall off. Yikes! "Careful!"

He pulls another tassel and we tilt to the left. He pulls another one and we go forward. "I did it!" he shouts. "We're moving forward!"

"Good job!" I say, even though we're moving *very* slowly. "Is there a tassel for speed? Or to go higher?"

"Um . . ." He pulls another one and we go up half a foot.

I quickly take off the ring, rub it, and Karimah pops out in the swirl of purple haze. The smoke strings blow a bit in the breeze from the slightly moving carpet.

"Hi!" she says. "What's up? You're using the carpet! Great!"

"Does this go any faster?" I ask. "Or higher?"

She shakes her head, her long pink hair swaying. "Probably not. I told you my magic isn't that strong."

"So this is the fastest and highest we can go?" I ask. We are now three feet off the ground. We are flying about the same speed that we can walk.

"I guess so," Karimah says. "Enjoy!"

I slide the ring back on and she disappears.

"At least we won't get any more blisters from walking," I say. And off we go.

chapter ten

Excuse Me

It takes us the same two hours to fly through the desert. Eventually we get back through the city gates, past the fountain, past the bigger houses, and then into the market.

"Um, excuse me, sorry," I say for the tenth time.

The problem with having a flying carpet that hovers only a few feet off the ground is that we keep bumping into people. Magic carpets must not be *too* unusual around here, because no one starts to scream when they see two kids and a dog on a flying rug. But people are annoyed by the constant bumping.

When we arrive at the street where Aladdin and his friends were playing duckball, a lot of kids are there. But no Aladdin. I hope his nose isn't *still* bleeding.

"Watch it!" says the girl with the dark brown ponytail when we accidentally knock into her with the carpet.

"Sorry!" I cry. "Hey, do you know where we can find Aladdin?"

"At his house," she says with a wistful look. "He's lucky. Do you want me to tell you how to get there?"

We nod and she gives us directions.

"Thanks!" I call out. "And sorry!" I can't help but wonder what she meant by *lucky*.

Aladdin's house is in an area with lots of narrow streets that crisscross and zigzag.

"Jonah, sharp right!" I warn him when a woman leading a white goat suddenly veers into our path.

"Got it!" he says, and turns left, but at least we didn't crash into them. "Abby?" he says, looking around. "I think we're here."

We see a small stone house that matches the description the girl gave us.

Okay. Now we just have to get Aladdin to listen to us.

But I have a plan.

We pull over and hop off the flying carpet. Prince runs around in circles for a minute. I think someone is very happy to be back on the ground.

"Where do I park it?" Jonah asks. The carpet is still hovering by his knees.

"I don't see any carpet parking," I say.

"I wish I had a lock for it. I can't just leave it here. What if someone takes it? Who wouldn't want a magic flying carpet?"

"Just roll it up," I say. "It's not that big. You can carry it under your arm like Mom does with her yoga mat."

"Oh, yeah," he says. He pulls one of the tassels toward the ground, and the carpet drops down. Then he rolls it up and stuffs it under his arm. "All set. Good carpet," he says, patting it.

We walk up to the house and I knock on the door.

A woman answers. She's around my mom's age, with curly black hair and dark eyes. She's wearing a long blue dress and blue slippers. "Can I help you?" she asks.

"Hi," I say. "You must be Aladdin's mom. I'm Abby and this is my brother, Jonah. Oh, and that's our dog, Prince," I add, glancing at Prince, who is sniffing the air. It smells like something delicious is on the stove.

"Welcome," Aladdin's mom says. "My name is Nada. Aladdin is inside. Come on in."

We walk into a small living room with a tattered gold-colored couch, a rocking chair, and a small wooden table. There's a thin, faded blue rug on the floor and purple patterned throw pillows. The walls are covered with family photos. Aladdin as a baby. Aladdin with his mom. His grandparents on their wedding day. The house feels well worn and well loved.

His mom sits down at the table in front of a bowl of carrots. She starts peeling one. "Aladdin, your friends are here."

Aladdin is lying on the couch with an ice pack on his nose, reading a book. He glances at us and sits up. "Hey, you're the girl and boy — and dog — from the duckball game. You're the one who hit me with the duckball!"

"I am so, so sorry," I say, flushing. "Are you okay?"

"I'm fine," he says. He takes the ice pack off his nose to show us a small red bump. I wince. "A little bruised, but no big deal."

I exhale in relief. "I'm Abby, by the way."

"I'm Jonah," my brother says.

"Is that why you came by?" he asks. "To apologize?" He puts a string bookmark in his book and closes it.

I'm suddenly reminded that I gave up on my tenth book for the read-a-thon to come here and I STILL can't help Maryrose at all. Maybe there's still a way, though. I have to keep trying, right? But for now, I really have to focus on the mess I made of this fairy tale.

Aladdin is staring at me.

Oops! Focus, Abby! "No! I mean, yes, of course I wanted to apologize, but actually, we're here because we'd like to introduce you to someone," I say.

"Who?" he asks.

"The princess," I tell him.

"Jasmine!" Jonah cries.

"No," I tell my brother. "That's not her real name, remember?"

"Princess Badr-al-Badur?" Aladdin asks.

"Yes! Do you like her?" I ask.

"Do I LIKE her?" Aladdin repeats. "She's amazing! I've never met her, but she's always doing good things for the village. She volunteers at the medical clinic and had a library built and stocked with books. We don't have a school, but I hear she's working on that."

Wow. She sounds like a really great person.

"What would you say if I told you that you and the princess were going to fall in love and get married?" I ask.

Aladdin starts laughing so hard that he falls off the couch. Even his mother is chuckling.

"What?" Jonah says. "What's so funny?"

"Hello?" Aladdin says. "I'm just a guy from the village." He lifts his foot. "I have holes in my sneakers. Dirt on my cheeks. At the moment, I even have a bruised nose. The princess would never fall in love with me. I have nothing." He laughs again. "You're funny, though."

"That can't be true," I say. "The girl you were playing duck-ball with called you lucky. Why are you lucky?"

He blushes. "She meant that I was lucky to have a mother. And a house. She's an orphan. A street kid. She sleeps at her aunt and uncle's house, but they don't really want her there. She spends most of her time hanging around the streets."

"Oh," I say. "You are lucky, then."

"And you're going to get even luckier," Jonah puts in.

"That's true," I say. I glance at my ring. "I'll tell you what," I add. "If you come with us to meet the princess and all goes according to plan, you can keep our genie."

Aladdin's dark eyebrows shoot up. "What plan? What genie?"

81

"Well, if everything works out and we can get back to our home, you can have this magic ring. A genie lives inside it and she grants wishes."

Aladdin doubles over in laughter again and slaps his knee. "You guys are hilarious. You should have your own comedy show at the theater."

"Show him, Abby," Jonah says.

I slide the ring off my finger. I rub the side. The sparkly purple haze comes from the ring, and Karimah pops out. She's still wearing her silver jumpsuit. But this time her long pink hair is in a high ponytail.

"Say hi, Karimah!" I say.

"Oh, hello!" she says, nodding at Aladdin and his mother.

Their mouths hang open.

Aladdin's eyes are huge. "You really have a genie!" he says. "I've heard of genies, of course, but I've never seen one up close. Can she really grant wishes?"

"Yes! And if we give you the ring when we go home, then she'll grant YOUR wishes."

Aladdin crosses his arms over his chest. "Let me see her grant a wish."

Oops. "Well, she can't right now because she's already granted three wishes today. She has a daily maximum."

He rolls his eyes. "I'm not sure I believe you. I mean, a girl did just pop out of your ring in a cloud of sparkly purple, but still. I don't know."

"Believe them," Karimah says. Then she yawns and stretches. Maybe granting our three wishes today made her sleepy. I can relate. I put the ring back on my finger and she disappears.

Aladdin stares at the spot where Karimah was standing less than a second ago. "Wow! She's gone just like" — he snaps his fingers — "that."

"Told you!" Jonah says. "She's a real genie."

But how are we going to prove it if Karimah can't make a wish come true right now?

"Look," Jonah says, unrolling the flying carpet. "She made this for us!"

Of course! The magic carpet! Go, Jonah!

The carpet hovers a couple of feet above the ground.

Aladdin's face lights up. "Cool! I've always wanted one of those! Can I try it out?"

"Yes!" I tell him. "As long as you'll come with us to the palace to meet Princess Badr-al-Badur."

"Okay!" Aladdin says, rushing toward the door. "I'll come. Mom! I'm going to the palace! Be home soon!"

Nada stands up, a carrot in her hand. "You are absolutely not going out at this hour. It's dinnertime."

"But, Mom! You heard what they said. Look at the flying carpet! You saw Karimah! She's a genie and we're going to get to keep her!"

"Aladdin, your new friends seem very nice," Nada says. "And it was thoughtful of them to apologize for hurting your nose. And maybe they managed to come across a real genie. A genie who suddenly *can't* grant wishes," she adds skeptically. "But it's late and you haven't eaten. You can play with Abby, Jonah, Karimah, and the carpet tomorrow."

"But —" I start.

"No buts," Nada says.

I look at the clock on the wall. It's 8:00 P.M. I glance at my watch — it's 12:25 A.M. at home.

Jonah's stomach suddenly growls.

Nada smiles. "Are you hungry?" she asks, looking at both of us.

I'm starving. And Jonah is always hungry. We both nod.

"You will share our dinner," she says.

"Awesome," Jonah says. "Thanks!"

A little while later, we sit down at the table. There's a small plate of lamb stew that would be barely enough for my dad alone, and warm flatbread. Everything looks and smells amazing, but how can we eat their food when they have so little?

Jonah reaches his fork for the meat plate, but I put my hand over his.

"We're really not that hungry," I say even though my stomach is growling. "We'll just wait until we get to the palace tomorrow."

Nada smiles warmly at me. "I cannot let children go hungry," she says. "Please, help yourselves. I even have a small bone for your dog." She goes to the tiny kitchen area and returns with a bone. Prince happily gnaws away on it on the rug.

Aladdin's mom is really nice. I serve Jonah to make sure he won't take too much, then myself, then pass the plates to Aladdin. I notice he's careful to leave his mother a decent portion.

"This is so good," Jonah says. "It doesn't even need ketchup."

That's his ultimate compliment. Jonah is obsessed with ketchup.

When dinner is done, I look up at the clock. It's nine P.M. I look down at my watch. It's twelve thirty in Smithville. So five minutes at home *is* an hour here. I was right! That means half an hour at home is six hours here. And an hour at home is twelve hours here — half a day!

"What day is it?" I ask. It was a Wednesday at home.

Aladdin's mom raises an eyebrow. I guess it is a weird question. "Monday," she says.

Okay. I do the calculations in my head. If Jonah and I want to be home at six forty-five A.M., that's six hours and fifteen minutes from now in home time. If one hour at home is twelve hours here, then we have three full days and three hours left here.

That should give us plenty of time. Hopefully.

"Uh, Abby?" Jonah says. "If we're not going to the palace until tomorrow, where are we going to sleep?"

Good question. Maybe on the flying carpet. Sure, it's wobbly but so are waterbeds, right?

Nada eyes us. "You don't have a place to stay?" she asks.

"No," I admit.

"You will sleep here," she says.

Yes! "You don't mind?" I ask.

"It will be our pleasure."

86

"Thank you," I say.

Nada offers me a long, colorful nightgown, and Jonah a pair of Aladdin's pajamas.

"Comfy," Jonah says. "Do you think I can bring this home?"

I yawn-laugh. "We'll see."

Nada unrolls an extra mattress on the living room rug. Then she and Aladdin say good night and Aladdin climbs a short ladder to a small loft that holds only a thin mattress and a shelf with just one book. Nada goes behind a beaded curtain to her room.

Prince curls up on the rug with his bone. Jonah and I stretch out head to foot on the mattress. We haven't slept head to foot since we were in the story *Snow White*. I hope he doesn't kick me in the face again.

"So tomorrow we just introduce Aladdin and the princess and hope they fall in love?" Jonah whispers. He sounds unsure.

I swallow hard. It's true that in a lot of the fairy tales we go into, the characters *don't* fall in love. Sometimes that works out for the best.

But what if Aladdin's right? What if the princess won't even talk to him because he's so . . . not royal?

And what if Karimah's magic isn't strong enough to make jewels and a grand new palace? Aladdin will never win over the sultan. He'll never marry the princess. And it'll be all my fault.

"That's the plan," I say, trying to stay positive. I flop over onto my stomach. "I just hope they don't hate each other."

chapter eleven

Flowerpalooza

bright and early the next morning, we're off via flying carpet to the palace: me, Jonah, Prince, and Aladdin (oh, and Karimah, who's in my ring). It's a little squished, but we manage. I'm feeling much more rested and alert. Jonah did kick me in the chin twice in the middle of the night, but I was so tired I was able to fall right back asleep.

"Can't we just wish ourselves there?" Jonah asks now as we narrowly sideswipe a man leading two children down the road.

"Sorry, Mr. Donkib," Aladdin calls out with a wave.

Ruff! Prince adds.

"I don't want to waste wishes when we have transportation,"

I say. "Even if it's bad transportation. Besides, we're almost at the palace." I can see it in the distance.

We fly low through the village and swerve our way through the cobblestone streets and between date trees and even a few camels.

I can't help looking down and admiring my new outfit. I didn't know that Aladdin's mom was a seamstress, but she sewed us new clothes to wear this morning. I'm in a purple silky jumpsuit that almost looks like Karimah's silver one. Jonah's jumpsuit is dark green and the billowy material of the pants puffs out in the slight breeze as the carpet flies. Both of us have matching shoes that curl up at the toes. And Aladdin's mom gave me a drawstring purse and a pretty red flower to tuck into my hair.

Aladdin is wearing a spiffy outfit, too. His jumpsuit is dark blue with a gold belt and a gold vest. If you look closely you can see that the outfits are sewn together with leftover materials, maybe scraps from his mom's job. But from far away, you can't tell. I'm glad Aladdin dressed up to meet the princess. I'm sure we'll need to convince her to like him.

Jonah steers the magic carpet around some trees, and we come into a clearing. There's a golden walkway lined with tall palm trees leading up to the palace. The palace itself is massive and topped with gold domes and surrounded by lush gardens.

The magic carpet hovers behind a huge date tree near the golden walkway.

"So what now?" Aladdin asks. "Do we ring the doorbell?"

"Would they let us in?" Jonah asks, holding one of the carpet tassels in pause mode.

Doubtful. It's not as if the royal family knows us. And when they ask why we're here, we can't exactly come out and say we're matchmaking the princess and a poor villager.

"I think we need Princess Badr-al-Badur to come outside," I say.

"But how?" Jonah asks. "Should we throw pebbles at her window or something?"

"If a villager throws rocks at the palace, he'll get arrested for sure!" Aladdin says.

"Okay, no pebbles," I say. "But let's see if we can find her room."

"Hey!" Aladdin says. "I think that's her." He points to one of the lower towers. I can make out a room with an open window. There's a beautiful girl with long dark hair covered by a pretty purple veil, packing her purse.

"She'll never talk to me," Aladdin says, frowning. "Even with my fancy outfit. I have nothing to offer her."

I have an idea. What if Karimah could whip up something nice for Aladdin to bring to the princess? Something like flowers?

I'm about to slide off my ring when I realize that will use up one wish. That means we'll only have two more for today. But Aladdin can't woo a princess empty-handed.

I slide the ring off, rub its side, and out pops Karimah. This time, her pink hair is in two pigtails.

"Karimah, I wish for flowers that Aladdin can give the princess."

Karimah bites her lip. "I'm sorry. I don't think I'm powerful enough to create flowers from scratch."

"But you made the flying carpet from scratch," I say.

She blushes. "No I didn't. I transformed the tablecloth that was under the lamp. No one was using it anyway."

I look down at the flying carpet. "Oh! I thought it looked familiar!"

"What about the flower in Abby's hair?" Aladdin asks. "Can I give her that?"

Jonah makes a face. "I don't think that one wimpy flower is going to do it. We need more."

"I know a multiplying spell I can try," Karimah says.

"Go for it," I say. "That's my wish."

Karimah stares at the flower in my hair. *"Flower, flower at this hour, I hereby ask you to use my power . . . and"* — Karimah stops and wiggles her fingers at the flower — *"multiply!"* she adds.

A rose pops onto the flying carpet. It's not the same flower as the one in my hair, but who doesn't love roses? Karimah's the best. Everyone should have their own genie, I tell you.

"It's working!" Jonah says as a daisy appears on his lap.

"Thanks, Karimah!" I say, sliding the ring back onto my finger. Karimah disappears. An orange iris lands on my foot. Wow, that's a pretty flower.

Then a yellow tulip appears.

And a tall sunflower.

And two more roses, pink and red. Then three more irises. Five more red roses. At least twenty black-eyed daisies. Then so many pink roses pop onto the carpet that I can't see Prince anymore. He's buried in roses! And the flowers keep coming. I'm already covered up to my waist! They're spilling over the sides!

"Stop the flowers!" Aladdin says. "I can't see!"

"Abby!" Jonah shouts. "Stop the flowers!"

"I can't!" I cry. "If I wish for the flowers to stop coming, I'll waste a whole wish! We only have two left!"

"But we're going to drown in flowers!" Jonah yells as a yellow daffodil lands on his head.

Sigh. I slide the ring off and rub it. Karimah appears through a cloud of purple haze.

"Karimah! I wish to stop the flowers from coming."

A white rose hits me in the chin.

"Sorry!" Karimah calls out. "I'm not so great at spells yet. I'll try my best." She stares at the flower in my hair and says, *"Flower, flower, at this hour, I hereby ask you to use my power and"* — she wiggles her fingers again at the flower — *"stop multiplying!"*

The flowers stop! Karimah did it! I thank her and slide the ring back on, and Karimah — *poof* — disappears back inside.

But the giant piles of flowers are still *everywhere*.

"Abby! I can't *seeee*!" Jonah cries. He's knocking long sunflowers out of his way, but there are so many.

The flying carpet is wobbling all over the place. It's heading straight for the castle.

Ahhh!

We're going to crash!

chapter twelve

How Sweet It Is

"ARGH!" we all scream as the flying carpet goes right through the open window and straight into the princess's sitting room.

The carpet stops short and we fall off. Flowers are scattered all over the couches and tables.

Uh-oh. Not exactly the plan.

The princess is standing up, her jaw dropped. Her purple headdress matches the long, lavender patterned dress she's wearing. She also has a pretty lavender purse on her arm.

Please don't arrest us, please, please, please.

"We're sorry!" I say immediately. "We didn't mean to fly in here! Please don't call the police."

"Of course I won't call the police," the princess says. "You brought flowers. A lot of flowers. I love flowers."

"Oh, good!" I say. "That's great! We're so glad we crashed into your room, then!"

"I was just on my way out the door," she says. "But really. How could I call the police on two kids with flowers?"

"There are actually three of us plus a genie and a dog," Aladdin says from beneath a pile of tulips.

Aladdin pushes the flowers out of the way and stands up.

The princess's dark eyes widen. "Hello," she says.

"Hello," Aladdin says back.

They stare at each other. And stare.

"Um . . ." I say. "Do you guys know each other?"

Neither of them answers. They just continue to stare.

"Guys?" I say.

The princess smiles. "No, I don't think we've ever met. I'm Princess Badr-al-Badur."

"Hello," Aladdin says. "I'm Aladdin."

They're still staring at each other. Their eyes are like magnets.

"I . . . I . . . I've always admired you," Aladdin says. His cheeks turn red. "I mean the good things you do for the village and the street kids and for animals, too."

Princess Badr-al-Badur grins. "I like to help people. And cats and dogs," she adds, bending down and brushing two pink roses off Prince's back. She pats his head, and Prince lets out a happy bark.

"I . . . I . . ." Aladdin keeps stammering, staring at the princess with moony eyes. "I should clean up these flowers and put them in a vase for you," he says.

Before Jonah and I can even introduce ourselves to the princess, she and Aladdin are huddled over the flowers, picking them up together. They sure are taking their time. The princess picks up a flower, and looks at Aladdin shyly. He turns red, and smiles. Then he picks up a flower, hands it to her, and she says, "For me?" while slowly batting her eyes.

Oh, brother.

But wait! This is perfect! This is exactly what's supposed to happen. They like each other!

A half hour later, still deep in conversation, Aladdin and the princess have all the flowers picked up. I would have offered to help, but every time I stepped forward, Aladdin

97

would hand the princess another flower and say something about how it couldn't possibly match her beauty. Then the princess would hand Aladdin ten flowers and say that he was as sweet as roses.

They're pretty adorable.

Finally, Aladdin stands. "Princess Badr-al-Badur," he says. "I . . . I . . . I . . ."

"Yes?" the princess asks, smiling.

"I think I love you," Aladdin says, his cheeks turning red.

"I think I love you, too," Princess Badr-al-Badur responds. She stands up beside him, beaming.

Jonah and I look at each other.

"Did that just happen?" he asks me.

"I think it did," I say. I glance at Aladdin and the princess. "Did you two just fall in love?"

They both nod.

"That's amazing!" I cheer. "Love at first sight!"

Jonah elbows me in the side. "But that's never happened before in fairy tales!"

"Well, it's happening now!"

Ruff! Prince agrees, looking from Aladdin to the princess.

Aladdin gets down on one knee, with a red rose in his hand. "Princess, do you want to marry me?" he asks.

The princess grins. "Yes," she says. "But you have to ask my father, the sultan, for permission."

"What's a sultan?" Jonah asks.

"'Sultan' is another word for king here in Mamlaka," the princess explains.

Aladdin gulps, then nods. He stands up. "Then that's what I'll do. I'll ask your father for permission. Let's go."

"We can't now," the princess says. "He's very busy this morning. But he'll be in the Great Hall this afternoon." She frowns. "Aladdin? What's wrong? You look worried."

"I am, Princess," he says. "Why would your father say yes? I have nothing to offer him. Nothing to offer you," he adds, hanging his head.

"Except love," Princess Badr-al-Badur says. "That is the most important thing."

"I'm not so sure the sultan will agree," Aladdin says.

"I have an idea!" Jonah pipes up. "We can bring the sultan all these flowers." He gestures around the room.

"Nice thought," the princess says. "But my father is allergic to flowers."

"Oh," Jonah and I say at the same time.

"He likes jewels," the princess says. "Do you have any gold, or some diamonds you can offer him?"

I'm about to say no when suddenly I remember: the jewel-fruit in my pocket. Yes! I'm so happy I risked OR ELSE to take a few.

"I have these," I say. I reach into my pocket, then hold out my hand with the three jewel-fruits on my palm.

Suddenly, something furry and brown takes a flying leap toward me and eats the jewel-fruits right off my hand.

"Prince, no!" I cry.

My palm has nothing on it but dog drool.

I hear Prince chomping away on the hard jewel-fruits as if they're crunchy dog biscuits.

And just when he was starting to behave again.

Jonah wags his finger at Prince, who's licking his lips. "Bad dog!"

Prince lies down and at least looks guilty.

"Now what?" Aladdin says.

I look at Aladdin and the princess, then at the ring on my finger. "Now we call in the genie."

chapter thirteen

The Sultan

Princess Badr-al-Badur has to leave because she's scheduled to bring toys to sick children. We go outside the palace gates and watch as she drives off in her horse-drawn buggy.

I slide the ring off, rub it, and Karimah pops up in her purple haze.

"Hey, guys!" Karimah says. "Did it work? Did the princess talk to Aladdin?"

"She did," Aladdin says. "She even agreed to marry me. But unless I can offer her father gold or jewels, he'll tell me no. Can you help?"

Karimah bites her lip. "I can try. But then you'll be out of wishes for today."

"Already?" Jonah says. "It's not even noon!"

I nod. We have no choice. We have to use our last wish of the day for the jewels. Or the king will tell Aladdin he can't marry the princess.

"Here we go," I say. "Should I just wish for a bag of jewels?"

"No," she says. "That's a two-parter."

"A what?" I ask.

"A two-parter," Jonah explains, nodding. "A bag of jewels. A bag. Of jewels. Two parts."

"Seriously?" I ask.

"Sorry," Karimah sighs, the smoke strings connecting her to the ring blowing a bit in the breeze. "I wish I had stronger magic."

"Oh!" I say. "I have the bag Nada gave me. Let's use that for part one."

"Great," Karimah says.

I open the silky purple purse.

"Okay, Karimah, I wish for jewels or gold *inside* this purse," I say, then hold my breath.

Please work. This has to work.

Karimah nods. "Got it."

"Maybe we'll get a million jewels!" Jonah says. "Like the flowers! We could take some home!"

Karimah takes a deep breath and stares at the bag in my hand. *"Rubies, emeralds, diamonds, and gold, give us something pretty to hold!"*

A poof of sparkles comes out of the bag. Yay! Something's happening!

Aladdin jumps up and races over. I open the purse wide. We all look inside.

It's not rubies. It's not emeralds. It's not diamonds and it's not gold.

Tsik-tsik, says whatever's inside.

Prince runs over and sniffs at the bag. *Grr-ruff! Grr-ruff-ruff!*

Jonah's eyes pop wide open. "It's a squirrel!"

I stare at the tiny, gold-colored, furry creature in my purse. "A squirrel," I repeat. "A teeny, tiny squirrel."

"Oops," says Karimah, her face scrunching.

"How did this squirrel end up in my purse?" I wonder aloud. "What does a squirrel have to do with jewels and gold?"

Jonah reaches a finger into my purse before I can tell him not to. But the squirrel seems happy and nuzzles against Jonah's finger.

"I think it's a *golden*-mantled ground squirrel!" Jonah says. "We just learned about them in school! And Karimah had the word gold in her rhyme . . ."

You've got to be kidding me. Then I notice the squirrel has a little gold collar with a name tag.

"'Goldie,'" I read. "The squirrel's name is Goldie."

"I'm *really* sorry," Karimah says, frowning. "I don't know what I did wrong. I'm just not good at making something out of nothing."

"We can take him home, right, Abby?" Jonah asks, using his pinky to pet Goldie's head. "He's so adorable. And Prince will learn to love him."

I look at Prince, who is staring at the squirrel with narrowed eyes.

"How will we explain to our parents why we have a squirrel?" I ask.

Jonah frowns. "The same way we explained Prince?"

I shake my head. "We have to at least try and give him to the sultan." But who wants a mini-squirrel? If Karimah had to zap up an animal, couldn't she have zapped up a golden retriever? Or a golden elephant?

"What if the sultan hates animals?" Aladdin asks. "Or if he's allergic to them? If only Princess Badr-al-Badur were here to ask."

I take little Goldie out of the bag and hold him close to my chest. He wiggles against me and licks my thumb. Awww, he's twitchy, but cute.

"Who could hate a squirrel?" Jonah asks.

Grr-ruff! Prince barks, trying to jump up on me.

"Our dog, for one," I say.

"Down, Prince!" Jonah scolds. "Be nice to the squirrel."

Prince listens to Jonah and sits. It's a start at least.

I put a squirming Goldie back in the bag, careful to leave it open enough so he can breathe. I put my ring back and Karimah disappears.

I climb back on the magic carpet and motion for Aladdin, Jonah, and Prince to do the same.

Goldie is all we have.

*   *   *

105

When we arrive at the Great Hall on the other side of the palace, there is a long line of people out the double doors. Are they all waiting to see the sultan?

Aladdin, Jonah, Prince, and I hop off the magic carpet. Jonah tucks the rolled-up carpet under his arm. I have the bag of squirrel. Aladdin is pacing at the end of the line. I'm not sure if animals are even allowed in the palace, so I tell Prince to wait for us behind a tree. He curls up to take a nap. I have to say, Jonah's doing a decent job of training Prince to be good. Besides the jewel eating, of course.

We wait for an hour in line. We slowly inch up in the marble hallway. It's impossible to tell what the other people are asking for. Hopefully, no one else is asking to marry the princess.

Finally, there's only one person in line in front of us. One minute later, the door opens and the guard gestures for us to enter.

"Come in!" booms the voice. A man sits on a throne at the opposite end of the room. He's wearing a white turban on his head and a long white robe. The top of his throne is actually inscribed with the word *Sultan*.

Standing just behind the sultan is another man, wearing a

dark green robe and a white turban. He is not smiling. Two guards stand on either side of the throne.

Aladdin lets out a breath. "I'm nervous," he whispers to me.

"Maybe the sultan will think love is all that matters," I tell him.

"Why do I doubt that?" he asks, looking around.

I see what he means. The Great Hall is lined with jeweled things, from tall gold vases to paintings with frames encrusted with rubies and emeralds and diamonds. Even the golden carpet leading to the king is dotted with jewels.

"You have to try!" I say. If you don't try, guess what. Nothing happens. "You've got this, Aladdin!"

He takes a few steps toward the throne. "Um . . . Hi? Mr. Sultan? I'm Aladdin. And I . . . would like to ask for your daughter's hand in marriage?"

The sultan raises an eyebrow. "My daughter?" he asks. "The princess?"

Aladdin nods and looks down at the floor.

The sultan studies Aladdin. The man standing behind the sultan leans down and whispers in his ear. Do I hear the words *poor villager*? I think I do.

Aladdin clears his throat. "Mr. Sultan? I mean, sir? I mean Your Highness. I love Princess Badr-al-Badur, and it's my greatest wish to marry her."

"I don't think so," the sultan replies. He starts to wave his hand to dismiss us.

"Wait!" I cry out. "Aladdin really loves the princess. And she loves him. Sure, they fell in love really, really fast, but they're going to be happy together. I promise."

"Do you have something to offer the sultan?" the unsmiling man asks. "Something of monetary value? A gift?"

Kuk-kuk! squeaks Goldie from inside the bag.

The sultan eyes the bag. "Is that for me? What is it?"

I take the teeny-meeny squirrel out of the purse and put it on the floor. "A golden-mantled ground squirrel?"

Muk-muk! cries Goldie.

A hush comes over the Great Hall. Everyone is staring at the tiny squirrel with the gold collar.

Oh, no. Did we break some sort of rule? Are animals really not allowed inside the palace? I figured Prince would have to wait outside, but this itty-bitty squirrel can fit in my pocket!

The sultan stands up. The man behind him steps forward and narrows his eyes at us again. The guards step forward.

I wait, holding my breath.

"Uh-oh," Jonah whispers.

"Uh-oh is right," Aladdin says. "I can forget about marrying the princess."

Kuk! the mini squirrel says. *Kuk-kuk.* Then he scurries over to the sultan and hops up onto his long purple slipper.

My eyes widen. We are SO about to get kicked out.

The sultan lifts up his foot. The little squirrel stretches and fluffs up his bushy tail over the edge of the slipper.

The sultan opens his mouth and . . . "Awww!" he says. "I've never seen a squirrel like this! Look at its stripes! And its adorable cheeks! I had a pet squirrel as a child, you know." He scoops up Goldie and cuddles him against his cheek. The squirrel licks his face and the sultan laughs.

Our offering is working! The sultan loves the tiny squirrel. Go, Karimah!

The sultan nods and nuzzles the squirrel, then notices the name tag. "And his name is Goldie! I love gold! Thank you!"

Aladdin boldly steps forward. "Sir Sultan? Is there any way you would consider my request now? To marry your daughter?"

The sultan whispers to the man beside him. Wait a minute. The man must be the vizier! The sultan's helper. I remember from the original story that the sultan's helper secretly wants the princess to marry his own son.

"I tell you what," the sultan says to us after he listens to the vizier. "We will approve the wedding, but you need to give us more than just a squirrel."

"You need to bring actual gold or jewels," the vizier says. "Forty buckets of jewels carried by eighty beautifully dressed marchers in a parade. Bring them on Thursday at noon."

"Then and only then can you marry my daughter," the sultan adds.

I'm pretty sure that's the same thing the sultan asked for in the original story.

But in the original story, Aladdin had the real genie. And we have . . . a rookie genie.

I think about all the jewels Karimah will have to zap up. She couldn't even come up with one bag of them!

"What are you waiting for?" the vizier snaps. "You are dismissed."

chapter fourteen

Back to the Cave

by the time we get back to Aladdin's house, it's midnight here. Aladdin's mom opens the door and hugs us all.

"I was so worried!" Nada says.

"Sorry," Aladdin says. Then his face breaks into a huge smile. "But the princess agreed to marry me!"

"What?" Nada's mouth drops open. "That's wonderful! I can't believe the sultan allowed it. Wow!"

"Um," I say. "About that. The sultan has demanded forty buckets of jewels carried by eighty marchers."

"Where are we going to find eighty marchers?" Jonah asks.

I have NO idea.

"It's late," Aladdin's mom tells us. "I say you all go to bed and wake up fresh in the morning to figure things out."

Jonah and I get back into our bed, head to foot. Prince is curled up on the rug beside us.

"I'll try not to kick you in the chin again," Jonah says.

"Try very hard, please," I reply.

"Abby? What are we going to do? Can Karimah even make ONE bucket of jewels?"

I turn onto my stomach. Jonah immediately kicks me in the shoulder.

"Oops, sorry!" he says.

Forget it. I can't fall asleep. I slide the ring off and rub its side. Karimah appears in the purple haze. She's wearing a gold jumpsuit, and her long pink hair is now in two braids.

"Oh, hi!" she says. "Everything going okay?"

I explain what happened at the Great Hall. The sultan's demand. The deadline of Thursday at noon. Tomorrow is Wednesday. We'll only have a day and a half to pull this off.

Karimah starts biting her nails. I didn't know genies did that.

"I can't just zap up eighty people," she says. "Or forty buckets of jewels! I tried to zap up jewels and look what happened! I made a squirrel!"

Karimah looks miserable. She's now biting the nails on her other hand.

"Don't worry," I tell her. "We'll figure it out in the morning."

Jonah is already snoring.

"Okay," Karimah says. She looks relieved. "Good night."

I slide the ring back on my finger and Karimah disappears.

I stare at the ceiling. Yes, I assure myself. We WILL figure it out in the morning.

Because if we don't, Aladdin won't get his happily-ever-after.

And it'll be all our fault.

I feel something vibrating on my finger. Half-awake, I sit up and yawn. It's early morning and Jonah and Prince are both still asleep. My finger vibrates again. I look at the ring. It's shaking!

Is it Karimah? Trying to tell me something?

I quickly slide the ring off and rub it. She leaps out.

"Wake up wake up wake up!" Karimah cries, waving away the purple haze. She starts spinning around, a big smile on her face. "Abby, I figured it out. At least part of it. We need to go back to the cave!"

"The cave?" Where I burned my elbow? Twice? Where the evil magician tried to trap us forever? "I hate the cave. Why do we need to go back?"

"I can't make a jewel appear from nowhere. But I can multiply! Remember those jewel-fruits from the cave? We'll go get some more and then I'll multiply them!"

I jump up. "That is a great idea, Karimah! Brilliant!"

She winks. "A gem of an idea?"

I laugh. "Yes. An absolute gem."

"Is it my imagination or is the flying carpet going a little faster today?" Jonah asks as we coast through the desert.

I'm sitting up front with him. Aladdin and Prince are behind us. Prince's ears flap in the breeze. There was no ear flapping yesterday.

"It is!" I say. "And a little higher, too. You're definitely getting the hang of magic-carpet flying." We only bumped into two people on the way.

"So since I mastered that, can I wear the ring now?" Jonah asks.

"Not yet," I tell him. "You could lose it. But I'll let you try it once before we leave, 'kay?"

"You better," he says, yanking the left tassel of the carpet.

We hover at the entrance to the cave and all hop off. Jonah rolls up the carpet and tucks it under his arm.

"Can I go in?" Aladdin asks.

"Sure," I say. "You and I can go and Jonah will wait here with Prince."

"No way!" cries my brother. "I love the cave! I want to go back."

"Okay, fine, we all go," I say. "But we all have to be careful!"

"Why?" Aladdin asks, grabbing the handle to the hatch.

I explain about the evil magician and OR ELSE and the star that burned me.

"So no bumping laser stars!" Aladdin says. "Got it!"

"Let's go," Jonah says. "Prince, be on your best behavior!"

Ruff! Prince agrees. At least, I think he agrees.

At the bottom of the stone steps, we follow the short hallway to the first room. Jonah lets Aladdin go in first. He grins and holds a finger to his lips in a shush gesture at me.

We hear Aladdin yelp. "Why are there thousands of me?"

Jonah laughs and we follow Aladdin into the room of mirrors. "Hi, thousands of Aladdins! Hi, thousands of Abbys! Hi, thousands of Princes! Hi, thousands of me!"

I imagine thousands of Jonahs. There would be a worldwide ketchup shortage.

"Come on," I say. "We have to get to the room with all the fruit trees!"

Aladdin and Jonah wave good-bye to their thousands of selves.

I brace myself for the next room. Like last time, it's pitch-black except for white stars all across it.

"Aladdin, this is the really scary room," I whisper. "You have to zigzag your way through the laser stars."

Aladdin narrows his eyes at the room. "I've got this. For the princess!" he shouts, and goes charging in, bending, stepping, and arching like a superstar.

"He must really want to marry her," Jonah says before he zigzags his way through the stars.

Prince goes next. Then it's my turn. Step, bend, arch, I remind myself.

I step. I bend. I arch.

I come to the star that burned my elbow. I step very

carefully. I bend very carefully. I arch very carefully. Then I lift up and —

I'm through! I did it!

Finally, we all reach the room with the trees.

"Huh?" Aladdin says, looking around. "Where are the jewels?"

"You're looking at them," I say, pointing. There are at least ten trees with brightly colored shiny fruit dangling from the branches. "Those little red things aren't pomegranates — they're rubies!"

"And the little green ones that look like limes are emeralds," Aladdin says, rushing over to one of the trees.

I lean over. "And the lychees are diamonds!"

Aladdin plucks a low-hanging diamond. "Awesome!"

"Pick one of each jewel," I say, and we all get to work.

I hold out the bag that Karimah zapped up for us yesterday. Everyone drops their jewels inside. We have a diamond, an emerald, a ruby, an amethyst, and a bunch that I don't even recognize.

"I'm taking a few extra for my mother," Aladdin says. "She has so little and gives so much. And for my princess. These are beautiful but not nearly as beautiful as she is."

Jonah rolls his eyes at the last part. But I think it's sweet. Aladdin is in love!

"Okay, we've got enough," I announce. "Let's head back. Careful going back through the rooms!"

We make it through without any star burns. We race up the steps to the hatch and climb out.

Jonah unrolls the magic carpet, we pile on, and back we go through the desert to Aladdin's house. This time the carpet flies even a tiny bit faster and higher.

"I can't wait to show my mom the jewels," Aladdin says when we arrive at his little house. "Soon the kitchen will be stocked with food. And she can buy clothes for us instead of having to make them out of scraps." He smiles as he rushes inside to find his mom. I'm glad Aladdin took extra jewels for her. She deserves them.

Aladdin's mom made us breakfast this morning, which was porridge with dates in it. She didn't have enough for all of us. I tried to decline again, but Nada insisted on sharing their meager food. She's so kind. Even Prince got a leftover bone from last night's dinner.

My stomach growls.

"I'm hungry, too," Jonah whispers as we follow Aladdin inside the house. "Is it almost lunchtime?"

"Let's turn the bag of jewels into buckets of jewels first," I say. "Then we'll worry about what to have for lunch."

I slide the ring off and rub its side. Karimah pops out.

I hold out a shiny red ruby that looks like an apple. "Ready?"

"Oh, great! You got the jeweled fruit!" Karimah takes the little apple in her hands. "Here goes nothing."

Or everything, really.

She closes her eyes in concentration. *Fruit in my hand, give me more as I command!"*

Another ruby-apple pops into my hand. Then another. In seconds, my hands are full of rubies! Then little sapphire-blueberries cover the top of the rubies. Emerald-limes start covering the rug. Diamond-lychees start covering the tattered couch!

Yay! It's working! The entire room is filling up with jewels of every color imaginable!

"You did it, Karimah!" I say, and slip the ring back onto my finger. Karimah disappears.

Jonah scoops up a handful of brightly colored gems and cheers. "Yeah!"

Woof!

I bend down and see something round and blue in Prince's

mouth. Oh, no! He's going to try to eat the sapphire again. I don't think so, buster!

"No, Prince!"

I grab the sapphire-blueberry out of his mouth. It has bite marks in it. I realize I can squeeze the slobbery blueberry as if it's a real blueberry.

"Um, Abby?" Jonah says. "Do you smell something? Something really good?"

I sniff the air. I do smell something good. Like . . . fruit?

Oh, no. The room is filled with fruit. Real fruit!

"They aren't ruby-apples!" I cry. "They aren't sapphire-blueberries. Those aren't diamond-lychees. They are real fruit!"

"And bananas," Jonah says, pointing at the table. "And strawberries. And raspberries."

Oh, no. Now that I think about it, Karimah asked for MORE FRUIT — not jewels!

Aladdin and his mom come inside, their eyes wide. "What is going on?" Aladdin asks.

"At least we know what we're having for lunch," Jonah says, and pops a blueberry in his mouth.

chapter fifteen

Say What You Mean

We spend the next hour gobbling up fruit. Some fruits I've never even seen before. And who knew that tomatoes are a fruit? And pumpkins!

"Prince sure likes watermelon," Aladdin says, laughing as Prince chomps on a rind.

When we're all stuffed, we help Aladdin's mom put away the rest of the fruit. We fill up every bowl and cabinet and the whole icebox!

Then we go back into the living room, and my ring starts vibrating. I slide it off and rub it. Karimah pops out. Her eyes are red-rimmed and her cheeks are wet. She's sobbing.

"I can't believe I messed that up!" Karimah says, wiping away tears. "I can't do anything right!"

"Yes, you can," I tell her, patting her back. "Let's try again."

Karimah sniffles. "But I can only make two more wishes today! What if I mess up again?"

"Maybe you won't," Jonah says. "Did you see how good I'm getting at flying the carpet? And remember when Abby burned herself on the star in the cave? Twice? But then when she had to go in again to get the jewels, she made it."

Huh. Thank you, little brother.

Karimah stops crying. She wiggles her fingers and a tissue pops into her hand. After dabbing under her eyes, the tissue disappears. How much would I love to be able to do that?

"You know what, Jonah?" Karimah says, her face brightening. "You're right. Abby has made tons of mistakes since she got here, and she hasn't given up! And she messed up a lot!"

"Um . . . I think I like Jonah's compliment better," I say.

"Aladdin's happiness depends on how I do," Karimah says, suddenly determined. "I just need a really good rhyme."

I suddenly have an idea. "What if you don't have to rhyme?" I ask. "Maybe the rhyme is what's messing it up. Maybe you need simple, no-frills instructions. Maybe you need to just say exactly what you want."

"But rhyming makes it magical," she says.

"No, *you* make it magical," I tell her.

She beams. "I can try." She picks up a jewel-apple from the table. "Here we go. *Abby would like a roomful of jewels, please!*"

We wait.

Karimah holds out her hand. A ruby appears on her palm. Then another. Then two diamonds. A bunch of emeralds. As opals fill her hand, she holds out both to catch them. The table is suddenly covered with sapphires. And garnets on top. Pearls pop up on the windowsills.

Jewels are everywhere! They are appearing on the couch. On the chair. Under the dining table. They're not stopping.

I pick up a diamond and give it a squeeze. Yay! It does not spray lychee juice. "You did it!"

Karimah is grinning. "I did it! We did it! Woo-hoo!"

Aladdin and his mother rush out of the kitchen. They stare at the jewels filling every space of the room. The piles of diamonds, rubies, emeralds, pearls, sapphires, and every color jewel imaginable are leaving us with very little room to stand.

"We have to get out of the way! We're going to drown in jewels!" Aladdin says.

All of our feet are covered in jewels. The piles are growing to our knees.

"Let's go into the kitchen!" Jonah yells.

I slide my ring back onto my finger and Karimah disappears. We run into the kitchen and close the door. An emerald gleams on Prince's brown fur. He shakes his whole body and the emerald goes flying, but Jonah sticks out his hand and catches it.

"Catchers keepers," he says.

I press my ear to the kitchen door. "I don't hear anything," I say. "I think the jewels have stopped coming."

Aladdin opens the door a crack. Two rubies and a diamond spill inside.

"I think the sultan will definitely let you marry his daughter now," Nada says with a laugh.

We take the magic carpet to the market, where we find forty buckets. We stack the buckets on the carpet and fly back to Aladdin's house.

Then I realize we have to deal with our last problem.

The eighty marchers.

When we bring all the buckets inside, everyone starts filling them up with jewels. While we're working, I say, "How do we find eighty people who will help us?"

"We can pay them!" Aladdin says, grabbing another bucket.

"With what?" Jonah asks.

"With jewels!" I say, nodding at Aladdin. "And fruit! We have tons!"

"I know a lot of street kids," Aladdin says. "They would definitely help if we gave them food and jewels."

"Are the street kids the ones you were playing duckball with?" Jonah asks. "Do they live in the street?"

"Most do," Aladdin says. "A few have homes. But they're all even poorer than I am. We don't have a school or many ways to earn money. I bet they would love to be in a parade."

I cheer. "Then let's round up our marchers!"

We take the flying carpet to the street where we first saw Aladdin. Jonah and I are each carrying two bags of fruit. Aladdin has a pouch full of jewels. To be helpful, Prince is carrying an apple in his mouth. I don't think anyone will want a dog-chewed apple, but it's the thought that counts.

A bunch of kids are playing duckball. Most of them are barefoot.

"Hey!" Aladdin shouts. "Who wants fruit? Who wants to earn some jewels?"

The duckball game stops and everyone runs over. We're surrounded by kids! And then we have to make our circle even bigger because more kids come to see what's going on. Then more.

"Can you count them?" I ask Jonah. "Make sure there are eighty!"

As Aladdin explains to the kids what we need them to do, Jonah walks around, counting.

"Seventy-six, seventy-seven —" He stops counting. "There are only seventy-seven!"

"Jonah and I will march, too," I say. "That's seventy-nine."

A boy with brown hair and dark eyes steps forward. His shirt is so worn it's practically see-through. "My twin brother is over there on the wall, reading," he says. "If you give me two jewels, he'll come, too."

"Make that eighty!" Jonah says.

"Okay, everyone!" I call. "Meet us at Aladdin's house at eleven tomorrow morning!"

"Wait — Abby," Jonah says. "What about the clothes? The sultan said they have to be beautifully dressed."

Oh, yeah. "Who doesn't have a nice outfit?" I call out.

They all raise their hands. Gulp.

"This is the nicest thing I own," says a little girl wearing a ripped gray dress. "Do you like it?"

"It's . . ." I stall. It's not fancy enough for the sultan.

The market is closed. And there's no way Aladdin's mother, a seamstress, can make close to eighty beautiful outfits overnight. "Give me one minute," I say, and head over behind a tree.

I'll have to use my last wish of the day. But what choice do I have? The kids need beautiful clothes or our plan won't work.

I slide my ring off and rub its side. Karimah appears. Her yellow eyes are bright and she's smiling.

"Karimah? The eighty kids who will bring the jewels to the sultan are going to need new outfits. Can you make them all new outfits?"

"Can do!" she says. "You have one wish left today." She stands up tall.

"Remember, Karimah," Jonah calls over. "Be specific! No rhymes!"

"Got it!" she calls back. *The eighty kids in the palace parade should all get beautiful brand-new clothes and shoes!"*

The air shimmers. I peer out from behind the tree. All the kids are suddenly in sparkling new outfits.

"You're getting really good at this!" I tell Karimah.

She beams. "That was easy. I just transformed their old clothes into new ones. It wasn't something from nothing."

"Well, it worked!" I say.

All around us, the kids are oohing and aahing over their new clothes.

Jonah comes over with Prince. "Their clothes aren't going to turn back to rags at midnight, are they?" he asks.

"Huh?" Karimah asks nervously as she bites her nails. "Why would they do that?"

"Never mind," Jonah says. "Fairy tale joke."

I laugh, smile at Karimah, then slide the ring back onto my finger.

chapter sixteen

1, 2, 3, March!

*t*hat night, I briefly worry that the kids will take their loot and not show up.

But at eleven the next day, the kids arrive. Every one of them! Aladdin's tiny house and yard are filled with kids. Nada hands out fruit smoothies, which everyone devours.

Nada also made fancy new suits for Aladdin and Jonah and a beautiful pair of billowy green pants and a matching jacket for me. You can barely tell that the materials are leftovers. I love them. Comfortable yet elegant! My favorite take-home outfit from a fairy tale yet. Not that I can go home yet. First I have to make sure that Aladdin and Princess Badr-al-Badur end up together. Then we have to find the portal home. Or at least get Karimah to zap one up.

And, of course, Maryrose is still cursed . . . But first things first. Make sure the sultan gives his blessing for Aladdin and the princess to get married.

"Let's get the party started!" I say. "Ready, everyone? Line up!"

Outside, the kids pair with a buddy to form a long line. Each team carries a bucket of jewels. Jonah and I are partners, of course.

"Let's go!" Aladdin says, leading the parade. He starts marching down the road. Even Prince looks like he's marching.

Some of the kids start singing and everyone joins in. People come out of their houses and clap and cheer. A huge crowd lines the road toward the palace.

Karimah can't miss the parade — it's all thanks to her! I slide the ring off and rub it and she appears.

"Wow!" Karimah says, grinning. "Everyone looks great!" She smiles at the little girl who was wearing the ripped gray dress and is now in a beautiful purple one. "You look so nice!"

"I've never had a new outfit before," the girl says, beaming. "Thank you!"

Tears come to Karimah's eyes and she gives the girl a hug.

Grr-ruff! Grr-ruff-ruff!

Why is Prince growling?

Grr-ruff! He barks again, looking into the crowd watching the parade. *Grr-ruff!*

"I can't hear the song if you keep barking!" I tell him.

"Any chance I can wear the ring now?" Jonah asks, marching beside me.

I guess I have been hoarding it. "Okay," I tell him, and slide it off. "But be careful with it."

"Yay!" Jonah says, sticking out his pointer finger.

I slip it onto his thumb instead, but the ring is still a little too big. "Careful," I say.

Finally, we arrive at the palace. The sultan, the vizier, and a bunch of guards are all waiting outside the doors. What's that on the sultan's shoulder? I squint to see. It's the little squirrel! Goldie!

"There's Princess Badr-al-Badur!" Aladdin says, pointing at the balcony above the doors. He waves and she smiles and waves back.

The sultan looks pleased as he watches the marchers come to a stop. Good sign! He leans over and whispers something to the vizier, who is NOT smiling.

I see the vizier counting kids and buckets. "Thirty-eight, thirty-nine, forty buckets — of jewels," the vizier says.

Does he sound disappointed? He does!

"Seventy-eight, seventy-nine, eighty marchers," the vizier adds with a scowl. He is definitely not happy that we met the sultan's demands.

"Very good!" the sultan says, giving Goldie a nuzzle with his cheek. "Aladdin, step forward."

Aladdin gives us a big smile and steps forward. I look at the balcony and see the princess matching his smile.

The sultan holds up one of the jewel-apples. "I am very impressed by all the gems you brought. For that reason —"

The squirrel makes a *muk-muk* sound.

The sultan looks at Goldie. "What's wrong?"

Goldie sniffs the jewel. Then he sniffs it again. Then he takes a small bite out of it. His cheeks puff up as if they're filled with air.

Uh-oh.

The sultan looks more closely at the gem. "It seems this jewel has turned into an actual apple."

Huh?

Uh-oh.

"Why did you give me fruit?" the sultan asks.

How did THAT happen?

Jonah elbows me. "Abby! We have a problem!"

"No kidding!"

"We have *another* problem!" Jonah bites his lip and holds up his hands. "I lost the ring!"

Nooooo!

chapter seventeen

Put a Ring on It

ir Sultan!" I call out. "Can you give us just five minutes?
We lost something important. We'll sort this fruit thing
out. Be right back. Promise!"

We start walking back the way we came, our eyes on the
ground. I see sand. I see twigs. I see a gum wrapper. But no ring!

"I'm so sorry, Abby," Jonah sighs. "I really messed up."

"Don't worry, we'll find it," I say. Jonah was so nice about all
my mess-ups. I can't be mean about his.

Grr-ruff! Ruff-ruff! Prince is barking like crazy again. What
is with him?

Oh, no.

Standing not far from the palace is Dracul. The evil magician! No wonder Prince was growling before. He must have spotted Dracul in the crowd. Prince WAS being good — by trying to warn us.

"Mwa-ha-ha!" Dracul laughs, his hand in the air. He's wearing the silver ring. It glistens in the sun.

CRUMBS!

"Mwa-ha-ha!" he laughs again, staring right at us. "You fools thought you could trick ME? I don't think so." He rubs the ring.

Nothing happens.

He narrows his eyes and stomps his foot. "Come out again, you dumb genie!" he yells, pulling the ring off and examining it. He rubs it again.

Out pops Karimah in the purple haze.

"Ha! Well, hello again, genie girl," he says. "How many wishes do I have left today?

"Two," she says. Her yellow eyes are sad as she looks at me and Jonah. "He wished for me to turn all the jewels into fruit! I had no choice! I'm sorry!"

Dracul steps toward the crowd, which parts for him. Karimah is dragged along by the strings attached to the ring. She's wobbling all over the place.

The sultan glares at Dracul. "How dare you interrupt the parade!" he shouts.

But Dracul just smirks at the king. "Lovely palace," he says, staring at it. He looks up and sees the princess on the balcony. "And lovely princess."

"Arrest that man!" the vizier shouts, pointing at Dracul.

But just as the guards race toward the evil magician, Dracul quickly says, "I wish to move this palace and myself to my hometown in the kingdom of Baeid!"

"Wait!" I scream.

But the castle vanishes. The castle and the princess, too.

"I'm so sorry, everyone," Karimah says sadly. "But I must listen to my new master."

"Quiet, genie girl," Dracul orders. "You were supposed to take me to Baeid!"

"But where is the princess?" Aladdin asks, his voice frantic.

"She's in the palace — but ... um ... I don't think I got her all the way to Baeid," Karimah explains. "I think I only got her to Taeid."

Dracul stomps his foot and glares at Karimah. "You fool! I said BAEID! Baeid is on the other side of the world! Taeid is just a boring town a day's journey from here!"

"Sorry, Sir Dracul," Karimah says, frowning. "I'm new at —"

"I don't have time for your excuses!" Dracul shouts. "You're supposed to take me to the palace!"

They vanish.

For once, I'm really happy Karimah is a newbie genie. At least Princess Badr-al-Badur and the palace aren't on the other side of the world.

Except we still have a major problem.

We have to rescue the princess WITHOUT a genie.

chapter eighteen

The Big Rescue

ind my daughter!" the sultan shouts. "Immediately!"

The vizier bows. "If I may speak, Sultan. As the magician said, the town of Taeid is a full day's journey by horse."

"I want my daughter back NOW!" the king shouts. His dark eyes turn sad. "How did this happen?" he says, shaking his head. The golden squirrel on his shoulder gives him a comforting nuzzle.

"Sir Sultan?" I say. "If I could just explain."

The king and the vizier glare at me. Even Goldie looks angry. I tell them about the magic ring slipping off Jonah's finger and the evil magician finding it. And how he now has control of Karimah — *our* genie.

"Silence!" the sultan yells. "Guards, arrest that boy and put him in prison," he says, pointing at Aladdin. "He gave us fruit instead of jewels and now he is somehow involved in the kidnapping of my daughter!"

"No, that's not fair!" I cry.

"Silence!" the sultan yells again. "You and your brother have until nine P.M. to return the palace and the princess, or you," he says, jabbing at finger toward me, "and you," he adds, pointing at Jonah, "and YOU," he shouts, shaking his fist at Aladdin, "will all be KILLED." The squirrel licks his cheek. "Okay, fine," he says, pointing at Prince. "But not you. You're adorable."

Guards drag Aladdin off to the village prison since the palace and its dungeon are now a day's journey by horseback.

The vizier sneers at me and Jonah and Prince, then escorts the sultan into a carriage without wheels, which is lifted up and carried along the road by six men.

Jonah and I look at each other in a panic. We have to go to Taeid NOW.

*   *   *

"We don't even know how to get to Taeid," Jonah says as we hop onto the flying carpet.

"But at least we can fly there," I say. "Now that the magic carpet goes higher and faster, we can get to Taeid a lot quicker than a horse can."

I'm about to ask someone in the street for directions when Prince jumps into Jonah's lap.

Woof! Prince barks, sticking his nose on the tassel on the left side of the carpet.

"Bad dog!" Jonah scolds. "Prince, you've caused enough trouble. Go sit!" Jonah points at the back of the carpet.

Prince sticks his nose in the air and sniffs, then nudges the tassel on the left. *Ruff-ruff!* He sniffs again and grabs the tassel with his teeth.

"Hey!" I say. "I think he's tracking Dracul's scent!"

Ruff! Ruff-ruff! Prince yanks the tassel to the left.

"I think you're right!" Jonah says. "Not bad dog! Good dog! Show us the way, Prince!"

Prince barks again and holds on to the tassel with his teeth. We fly through the desert for over an hour and then Prince noses the tassel on the right. Jonah turns and we soar through another village.

A few hours later, Prince barks and moves to the left side of the carpet. *Woof! Woof-woof!*

"We're here!" Jonah says. "I see the palace up ahead in that clearing!" Jonah gives Prince a big scratch behind his ears. "Good boy! You did it!"

Ruff! Prince barks, puffing out his furry brown chest.

I squint in the hot sunshine. It's definitely the sultan's palace on a hill. A river surrounds it.

"Get closer so we can see what's happening," I say. "Do not, I repeat, do not, tip us over into the river. Who knows what's in there?"

"Got it!" Jonah says. "Do not fall into the river. OR ELSE!"

"Exactly."

We fly right up to the castle. "There's Princess Badr-al-Badur," I say, pointing at a window in the domed tower. The carpet is able to hover just up to the window.

"Princess!" I call out.

She rushes over and opens the window. "Dracul has proposed marriage," she cries. "He expects me to say yes! He thinks if we marry, he can take over the whole world! But I love Aladdin."

"We know!" Jonah says. "You can't marry that horrible Dracul!"

I think for a second. No, she definitely can't marry that truly evil magician. "Wait a minute!" I cry. "Tell him you *will* marry him!"

"What?" Princess Badr-al-Badur asks, her dark eyes nervous.

"Yeah, WHAT?" Jonah repeats. "Why would she accept that awful magician's proposal?"

"Because maybe she can get Dracul to give her the magic ring as an engagement ring!" I explain. "It's the only way to get the ring back from him."

"But I cannot tell a lie," the princess says. "To Dracul or anyone. It wouldn't be right."

Her eyes suddenly widen and she turns away. "I hear the doorknob turning. He's coming!"

Jonah inches the flying carpet back from view of the window. We listen hard.

"Princess," we hear Dracul say, "I must have your answer now. Will you marry me?"

"Um, well, I . . ." she begins. "Aren't you going to offer me an engagement ring upon proposing marriage?"

Jonah inches the carpet toward the edge of the window. We peer in.

Dracul is staring at the magic ring on his finger. "But how can I give you this ring, Princess? You will command the genie girl to take you home."

The princess shakes her head. "I promise not to do that," she says. "And a princess never breaks a promise."

"Well, if you promise." Dracul nods and slides the ring off his finger.

I wait, holding my breath.

He hands her the ring. He gets down on one knee to propose again.

"Abby, catch!" the princess calls out. She throws the ring out the window.

I stick my hand out. "Got it!" I cry. "Catchers keepers!"

Yes!

"Liar!" Dracul yells. "Promise breaker! You said —"

"I said I wouldn't wish myself home!" the princess interrupts. "That doesn't mean someone else can't!"

"Noooooo!" Dracul shouts, stomping his foot.

I rub the ring, and Karimah appears. "Bring the palace, the

princess, me, Jonah, and Prince back to the sultan's kingdom," I tell her. "And Dracul, too — in handcuffs!"

"As you wish," Karimah says with a wink.

Poof! Just like that, the palace and the princess are back where they belong. Well, the palace is a bit to the left of where it used to be, but close enough. The sultan, the vizier, and the guards are all waiting. I glance at the clock on the wall. It's 8:59 P.M. We did it with one minute to spare! PHEW.

The crowd of villagers cheers. The sultan looks happy. The vizier doesn't look happy, but he never does. The princess rushes over to her father and they hug.

I rub the ring, and Karimah pops out.

"You did it!" I tell her. "And that was a two-parter! You got the handcuffs, too. You rock as a genie!"

"Yay!" she says. And then she adds, "Some of the time."

"And you rock as a dog!" Jonah says, bending down to give Prince a hug.

"Arrest that evil magician!" the sultan yells. The guards grab the handcuffed Dracul and drag him into the palace to the dungeon.

"The dungeon better not be small," Dracul cries as he's carted off. "I'm very claustrophobic! And I get really hungry! I'm going to need granola bars!"

Jonah and I smirk at each other.

"Bring me Aladdin," the sultan commands.

Guards appear with Aladdin, who looks distraught. But when he sees the palace back where it was, his expression turns relieved.

The sultan calls for silence. A hush falls over the crowd. The sultan holds up one of the apples.

"Aladdin, you were not able to bring me the jewels that I requested."

Aladdin hangs his head. "I'm sorry, Sultan. I tried. I know I failed to meet your requests, but I want to say that I love your daughter. And I will make it my mission in life to be a kind, loyal, and supportive husband."

The sultan turns to the vizier. "What do you think?"

I hold my breath. Are we doomed?

Slowly, the vizier nods. "I believe him. He will make a good husband."

"I think so, too," the sultan says. "Aladdin, I grant you permission to marry my daughter. Welcome to the family!"

145

I can't believe it!

Aladdin is beaming. The princess is smiling. Everyone is cheering and clapping.

"Fruit for everyone!" the sultan exclaims.

"Um, Abby?" Jonah says. "I'm really happy for them, but we have one last problem."

We do? "What?" I ask.

"We're out of wishes for today. How are we going to get home?"

That IS a problem. But — if we can wait till midnight to leave, we'll get three new wishes when the clock strikes twelve! CAN we wait till then?

Okay, let me think. When it's midnight here, it'll be . . . six forty-five A.M. at home. We'll be pushing it, but we can make it! I decide not to think about the fact that my parents' alarm goes off at six forty-five. They could catch us rushing upstairs to our rooms. But I guess we have to try.

We also have to try and uncurse Maryrose before we go.

"Karimah?" I ask. "Now that you're so good at genie-ing, do you think you can free our fairy Maryrose? Not now, but as soon as the clock strikes midnight? If we wish it?"

146

Karimah shakes her head. "I'm really sorry. But my magic isn't big enough for that. Maybe in a hundred years, I'll have the power of the genie of the lamp. But not yet."

Crumbs. Double crumbs. "Well, at midnight we're going to wish ourselves home. Is that okay?"

Karimah nods. "Yes. Go back to the cave where we first met. See you just before midnight!"

I slide the ring back onto my finger.

Poof. She's gone.

We don't have that much time, but Jonah, Prince, and I take the magic carpet back through the desert to the mouth of the cave. Aladdin and Princess Badr-al-Badur come along to see us off. We get there exactly at eleven forty-five P.M.

"Do we have to go through all the rooms again?" Jonah asks.

I really hope not. We only have fifteen minutes.

I slide the ring off and rub it. Out pops Karimah.

She smiles. "I'll miss you guys," she says. "Your portal home is through the very first room in the caves — the room of mirrors. On my count of three, you'll see a swirl of purple.

147

Just walk right into one of the thousands of yous and you'll be home."

"Do you really have to go?" Aladdin asks.

"Yes, please stay as a guest of our kingdom," the princess says.

I glance at my watch. "I wish we could, but we have to go or we'll be in big trouble," I say. We have to get back home. And back to school. And to the final day of the read-a-thon. Sigh. I'll have to watch Penny win. Penny with her hundred dollars' worth of pennies. Groan.

I turn to Aladdin. "Well, Aladdin, I made you a promise and I don't break promises, either. So the ring is yours." I hand it to him.

He holds it in his palm. Karimah bows to him.

"I would like to make a wish," Aladdin says. "For the street kids, the ones who aren't as lucky as I am, to have a palace of their own."

"I'll do my best," Karimah says. *"Aladdin wishes for a palace for the street kids!"* Then she wiggles her fingers and a little scene bubble appears in a sparkly haze. We can see the road where the kids play and sleep. But a castle has appeared with domed towers of various heights. Where there was dirt is now a grassy meadow. Sleeping boys and girls wake up and cheer and race inside.

"I did it! I created something new!" Karimah cries, then wiggles her fingers, and the image bubble disappears.

The princess smiles. "I'm so happy for them. And us," she adds, smiling at her husband-to-be.

"Me too," Aladdin says. "The princess and I don't need anything else. We have each other and that is enough." He hands the ring back to me. "Thank you for inspiring me to reach for the stars. The princess is the brightest star I have ever known."

"Brighter than the laser stars?" I ask with a wink.

Aladdin laughs. "Much, much brighter."

"And I don't burn elbows!" the princess says.

Jonah cheers. "We get to take home the ring!" he says. "We'll have our own genie in Smithville!"

"Jonah, you know we can't do that."

Oh! Wait! I should wish for a spellbook! Something that will help us set Maryrose free!

"I have one more wish," I say. "It's that —"

But then I stop. Because if I only have one more wish, I know what I have to wish for. I smile at Karimah. "I wish to free Karimah from the ring!"

Karimah's eyes widen. Suddenly, there's a burst of purple haze and the strings tethering her to the ring disappear.

Karimah gasps and dances from side to side, front to back. "I'm free! I'm really free! Thank you so much!" she says to us.

"Do you still have magic powers?" Jonah asks.

"Yes!" Karimah says. "I have magic but no master. I make my own decisions. And all I want is to stay right here and help all those kids. Did I mention I love to cook? I can wish up the ingredients and make feasts every night!"

"Awww," I say. "That's really nice."

Jonah bites his lip. He seems to be thinking about something. He walks over to Aladdin. "I was going to ask Abby if we could bring this home, but I want you to have it after all." He takes the rolled-up magic carpet from under his arm and hands it to Aladdin.

Aladdin smiles. "Thank you, Jonah. The princess and I will have many adventures on it."

"Oh!" Karimah says. "It's one minute to midnight. You and Jonah and Prince had better hurry to the room of mirrors. One, two —"

"Bye!" Jonah and I say to Aladdin, the princess, and Karimah as I scoop up Prince in my arms and we rush down the stone steps into the room of mirrors. And then on Karimah's count of three, there's a swirl of purple and we step through together.

We're going home.

chapter nineteen

And the Winner Is . . .

Jonah and I step forward right onto the floor in our basement. Prince leaps from my arms.

It's six forty-five A.M.

Beep. Beep. Beep.

Oh, no! Our parents' alarm clock just went off.

But I have to talk to Maryrose. I look at the mirror. All I see is my reflection. "Maryrose? Are you there? Hello?"

The mirror ripples. A face appears in the glass. Maryrose's long wavy hair covers the carvings of fairies on the stone frame of the mirror.

"Maryrose! I'm so sorry we didn't free you," I say.

Are those tears in Maryrose's eyes? I step closer. Her eyes are definitely misty.

"Thank you both for trying to help me," she says. "I am very touched. But even the genie of the lamp wouldn't have been powerful enough to free me. It means a great deal to me that you tried. Thank you." The mirror ripples again and she's gone.

Maryrose was teary because we tried to help her. Wow. One day, I hope we actually CAN help her.

"Abby, we have to go!" Jonah says.

We rush upstairs, turn, and then dart up the next flight of stairs. We tiptoe past my parents' bedroom. I don't hear a thing.

"I think they hit the snooze button," I say.

As Jonah opens his bedroom door, I tap his arm. "Hey, Jonah."

He turns and yawns. "Yeah?"

"That was really nice of you to give up the flying carpet to Aladdin. I thought you might try to sneak it home."

He shrugs. "It would have been really cool to have it. But you freed Karimah from the ring, so . . ."

I smile and nod. He's a cutie.

"Prince, go lie down in your bed," Jonah says.

Prince wags his furry tail and pads over to his dog bed in the corner of Jonah's room. Then he circles around three times and plops down. In seconds, he's snoring.

"You did a great job training him, Jonah. Mom and Dad are going to be really happy."

He smiles. "Thanks, Abby. See you in a few."

He goes into his room and I go into mine. I quickly change out of the pretty outfit Aladdin's mom made for me and put on my pajamas.

I look at my hand and realize I'm wearing the silver ring. It doesn't have a genie inside it, but it's still pretty. I slip it off along with my watch and put both away in my jewelry box. Then I look at the drawings of fairy tale characters. Aladdin and Princess Badr-al-Badur are on the flying carpet, hovering near the kids' palace. Aladdin and the princess are smiling, and if I look closely in a window of the palace, I can just make out Karimah in the kitchen with a group of kids around her. They're all cooking something.

Awesome. I close the jewelry box and notice the book I left unread lying on my dresser.

I have a little time. I'm going to finish this book, even if I have no chance of winning the read-a-thon. Maybe trying is what matters — even if the end result isn't what you want. Like a squirrel instead of a bag of jewels. But sometimes that can be pretty great, too.

By the time my mom calls me down for breakfast, I've finished the tenth book. I'm not going to win the read-a-thon, but it was worth it — the book was pretty great!

When I get downstairs, I see Prince outside in the backyard with my mom.

"Kids?" my mom calls through the open sliding glass door to the kitchen. "What on earth did you give Prince to eat that was sparkly?"

Ruff! we hear Prince bark.

Jonah and I race over to the door. Our mom is holding a doggie poo bag and making a funny face at it.

Ruff! Prince barks again.

Jonah and I cover our mouths to keep from laughing.

I'll bet if Prince had a chance to ask Karimah for a wish, he'd request more jewel-fruit.

"I won! I won! Go, me!" Penny says after the principal made the read-a-thon winner announcement over the loudspeaker.

The good news was: The principal surprised everyone by deciding to choose two winners. The person who raised the most money, Penny, and the person who read the most books. That was a girl named Priya, who's in another class. I was glad about that. Because Penny winning just doesn't seem fair.

Not that life is always fair.

Maryrose is cursed to live in a mirror. That's definitely not fair.

"What books are you going to suggest to the librarian?" Robin asks Penny as we line up to head out.

"Well, I'm going to ask for some new books about horses," Penny says. "But if you and Frankie and Abby have any books you want me to ask for, I can do that, too."

My mouth drops open. Penny being nice? She's like the vizier — full of surprises.

Am I actually smiling at Penny? I am. I am smiling at Penny.

"I know what I want," Frankie says, pushing her red glasses up on her nose. "One book of ghost stories. And one about soccer."

"Two books on science for me," Robin says, putting an arm around Penny.

Penny is being so nice that I don't even mind that Robin and Penny have their hair in matching high ponytails again. I don't mind TOO much.

"Do you know what books you want me to ask for, Abby?" Penny asks me.

Sure do. "One book of fairy tales. And one book on spells."

Whaddaya know? I didn't even win the read-a-thon and the two books I want most will still be ordered.

And maybe, just maybe, I can find a way to uncurse Maryrose.

acknowledgments

Thanks to all! Especially:

Everyone at Scholastic: Aimee Friedman, Jennifer Abbots, Abby McAden, Olivia Valcarce, David Levithan, Tracy van Straaten, Bess Braswell, Caitlin Friedman, Antonio Gonzalez, Lizette Serrano, Emily Heddleson, Emily Rader, Elizabeth Krych, Rachael Hicks, Elizabeth Parisi, Sue Flynn, and Robin Bailey Hoffman.

Amazing agents: Laura Dail and Tamar Rydzinski.

Helpful genies: Deb Shapiro, Lauren Walters.

Second readers: Joy Simpkins, Chloe Swidler, Munawar Abbas, and Emellia Zamani.

Kelly McCloskey, for the title suggestion!

And to all my friends, family, supporters, and writing buddies:

Targia Alphonse, Tara Altebrando, Bonnie Altro, Elissa Ambrose, Robert Ambrose, Jennifer Barnes, Emily Bender, the Bilermans, Jess Braun, Jeremy Cammy, Avery Carmichael, Ally Carter, the Dalven-Swidlers, the Finkelstein-Mitchells, Alan Gratz, the Greens, Adele Griffin, Katie Hartman, Anne Heltzel, Farrin Jacobs, Emily Jenkins, Maureen Johnson, Lauren Kisilevsky, Leslie Margolis, Maggie Marr, the Mittlemans, Aviva Mlynowski, Larry

Mlynowski, Lauren Myracle, Jess Rothenberg, Melissa Senate, Courtney Sheinmel, Jennifer E. Smith, the Steins, Jill Swerdloff, the Swidlers, Robin Wasserman, Louisa Weiss, the Wolfs, Maryrose Wood, Sara Zarr, and the downtown bus families even though we're no longer on the downtown bus.

Special shout-out to Coco, Belly, and Todd: I love you.

And of course, thank you, Whatever After readers. I hope all your wishes come true.

DON'T MISS ABBY AND JONAH'S NEXT ADVENTURE!

Whatever After #10
SUGAR and SPICE

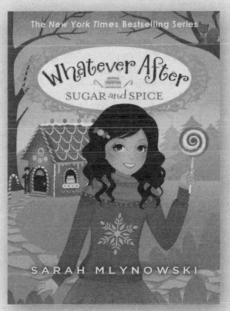

The *New York Times* Bestselling Series

Whatever After

SUGAR and SPICE

SARAH MLYNOWSKI

When Abby and Jonah get mixed up in Hansel and Gretel's story, they're the ones who end up trapped in the witch's cake house! Can the siblings avoid getting eaten, put everything right, and make it back to home sweet home?

"I'm tired," Gretel complains, frowning. "Your dumb dog is leading us on a wild dog chase."

"Yeah," Hansel says. He picks up a rock and tosses it at Prince, just missing.

"Hey!" I shout.

"So?" Hansel says. "It's just a dog."

"Just a dog?" I say. "What's wrong with you? And he's not dumb. Be nice to him!"

Gretel puts her hands on her hips. "Don't tell my brother what to do!"

Ugh. I swear I don't remember Hansel and Gretel being this awful in the original story.

Jonah and I aren't this awful, are we?

No. We can't be.

Maybe they're just really hungry. Who knows when the last meal they had was? Pieces of bread are not a meal. I can't blame them for not being in the best mood.

But . . . being hungry is not an excuse to throw rocks at dogs.

"Abby," Jonah says, pointing. "Look! A house!"

Up ahead, through some trees, is a totally adorable cottage. It's light pink with a light-brown roof. The windows are trimmed in red and white.

"That's not *our* house," Gretel says. "Our house is half the size and mud brown." She stares at the cottage. "The doorknob looks like a cookie. I'm so hungry my eyes must be playing tricks on me."

It does look like a cookie. A chocolate-chip cookie. And the trim around the strawberry-colored door looks like pie crust.

Because it *is* a chocolate-chip cookie. And it *is* a pie crust. It's the cake house!

We found it! I bend down and scratch behind my dog's ears. Good job, Prince!

Jonah lifts his nose and sniffs the air. "Do you smell strawberry shortcake?" he asks.

"And brownies?" Hansel says.

"And gingerbread?" Gretel says.

"Yup, yup, and yup," I say, smiling. "You're all correct. This, my friends, is the cake house."

Gretel's eyes almost pop out of her face, slinky style. "It's real?" she asks.

"Told you so," I say smugly. Take that, Gretel!

"Hunnnnnngry," Hansel says. "Want candy."

"Me too," says Gretel. "Come on, Hansel. Let's go!"

I grin at Jonah. We're here. Whew. Now the story can unfold exactly the way it's supposed to. Yay, us.

Hansel and Gretel start running down the hill. Hansel reaches the house first.

"It smells so good," Jonah says.

"It does," I say as the yummiest-smelling breeze ever wafts toward me.

"I'm just going to run up and take a little taste. 'Kay, Abby?"

Sniff. Yum. Sniff, sniff. "But . . ."

"I don't see the witch," Jonah says. "We'll be careful. Let's just take a closer look. We have to. It's a cake house! It's THE cake house."

Well . . . we'll have to be careful . . . but . . . if the witch doesn't see us . . .

My stomach is growling.

And I could really use some dessert.

And . . . it's the CAKE HOUSE!

I run down the hill.

Each time Abby and Jonah get sucked into their
magic mirror, they wind up in a different fairy tale —
and find new adventures!

Read all the
Whatever After books!

Whatever After #1: FAIREST of ALL

In their first adventure, Abby and Jonah wind up in the
story of *Snow White*. But when they stop Snow from eating
the poisoned apple, they realize they've messed up the
whole story! Can they fix it — and still find Snow her
happy ending?

Whatever After #2: IF the SHOE FITS

This time, Abby and Jonah find themselves in Cinderella's
story. When Cinderella breaks her foot, the glass slipper
won't fit! With a little bit of magic, quick thinking, and
luck, can Abby and her brother save the day?

Whatever After #3: SINK 'n' SWIM

Abby and Jonah are pulled into the tale of *The Little Mermaid* — a story with an ending that is *not* happy. So Abby and Jonah mess it up on purpose! Can they convince the mermaid to keep her tail before it's too late?

Whatever After #4: DREAM ON

Now Abby and Jonah are lost in Sleeping Beauty's story, along with Abby's friend Robin. Before they know it, Sleeping Beauty is wide awake and Robin is fast asleep. How will Abby and Jonah make things right?

Whatever After #5: BAD HAIR DAY

When Abby and Jonah fall into Rapunzel's story, they mess everything up by giving Rapunzel a haircut! Can they untangle this fairy tale disaster in time?

Whatever After #6: COLD AS ICE

When their dog, Prince, runs through the mirror, Abby and Jonah have no choice but to follow him into the story of *The Snow Queen*! It's a winter wonderland . . . but the Snow Queen is rather mean, and she FREEZES Prince! Can Abby and Jonah save their dog . . . and themselves?

Whatever After #7: BEAUTY QUEEN

This time, Abby and Jonah fall into the story of *Beauty and the Beast*. When Jonah is the one taken prisoner instead of Beauty, Abby has to find a way to fix this fairy tale . . . before things get pretty ugly!

Whatever After #8: ONCE *upon* a FROG

When Abby and Jonah fall into the fairy tale of *The Frog Prince*, they realize the princess is so rude they don't even *want* her help! But will they be able to figure out how to turn the frog back into a prince all by themselves?

Whatever After #9: GENIE in a BOTTLE

The mirror has dropped Abby and Jonah into the story of *Aladdin*! When things go wrong with the genie, the siblings have to escape an enchanted cave, learn to fly a magic carpet, and figure out WHAT to wish for . . . so they can help Aladdin *and* get back home!

Whatever After #10: SUGAR and SPICE

When Abby and Jonah get mixed up in Hansel and Gretel's story, they're the ones who end up trapped in the witch's cake house! Can the siblings avoid getting eaten, put everything right, and make it back to home sweet home?

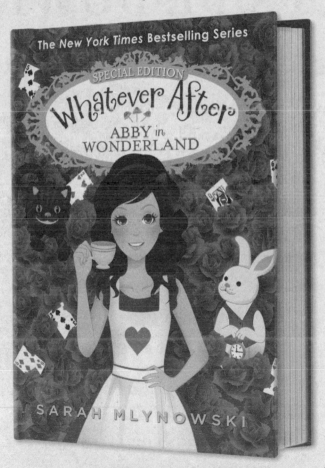

WHAT HAPPENS WHEN YOUR MAGIC GOES UPSIDE DOWN?

From bestselling authors
Sarah Mlynowski, Lauren Myracle,
and **Emily Jenkins** comes a series about
magical misfits who don't fit in at their school.